WORTH THE FIGHT

WORTH IT ALL
BOOK 3

LIZ DURANO

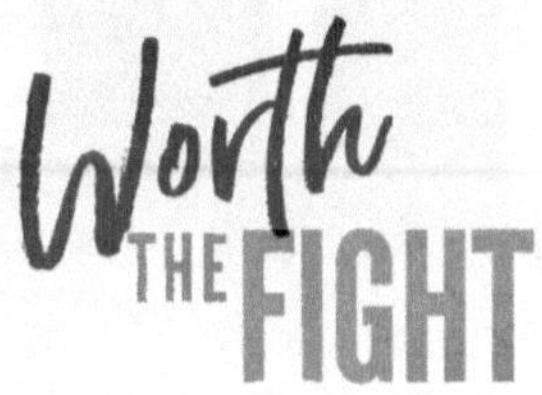

SHE HAS PLANS. HE HAS FOREVER.

At forty-one, Cassie Reynolds has a plan: finish her compliance contract at Pierce Enterprises and single motherhood through a sperm donor. No complications. No risk.

None of her plans included Elliot Walker.

Seven years ago, she was his mentor at Stanford. Now he's the CEO she's supposed to assess with complete objectivity —except there's nothing objective about the way he looks at her.

Getting involved could destroy both their careers especially when a board member bent on revenge is already watching for any sign of weakness.

But when professional boundaries blur into something neither can resist, Cassie faces an impossible choice: protect the reputation she spent twenty years building, or risk everything for a man who makes her want things she swore she'd never want again.

1

Cassie

Single. *Married. Widowed. Partnered.*

I stare at the options, as if I can't decide what to check off. As if I don't know what I am, have been for the last three years.

Across from me, a woman—mid-thirties, wedding ring, holding her husband's hand—glances my way, her look quick before she turns away. I know that expression too well. I've seen it at work, at family gatherings, in coffee shops when I'm sitting alone.

Single. Married. Widowed. Partnered.

I check the correct box with more force than necessary. Single.

"Cassandra Reynolds?" A nurse appears at the doorway, clipboard in hand, her smile professionally warm. "We're ready for you."

I follow her down a hallway decorated with soft water-colors of mothers and babies—all strategically diverse, all glowing with that impossible luminescence that only exists in stock photography. We pass examination rooms with their paper-covered tables and stirrups that remind me exactly how undignified this process is about to become.

The consultation room is better. A desk, comfortable chairs, a window overlooking the San Francisco streets below. Dr. Madison Rowland rises to greet me—early forties, confident handshake, the kind of competence that costs four hundred dollars for thirty minutes.

"Ms. Reynolds, thank you for coming in." She gestures to the chair across from her desk. "I've reviewed the preliminary bloodwork and your health history. Everything looks good for proceeding with treatment."

Treatment. Such a clinical word for what I'm trying to do. Create life. Become a mother. Do the thing I've wanted since I was thirty and kept pushing off because the timing was never right, because Brad kept saying "soon," because I believed him.

"Let's talk about your options," Dr. Rowland continues, pulling up charts on her computer screen. "Given your age—"

"Forty-one," I say. Might as well own it.

"Forty-one," she agrees without judgment in her voice. "Your AMH levels are actually quite good, which is encouraging. We have several paths forward. IUI—intrauterine insemination—is less invasive and less expensive, but success rates at forty are around fifteen to twenty percent per cycle. IVF offers higher success rates, approximately thirty to forty percent per cycle, but it's more intensive and significantly more costly."

She walks me through the numbers. The percentages. The protocols. The medications that will turn my body into a hormone factory. The monitoring appointments. The two-week waits. The very real possibility of failure, again and again, until my savings run dry or my body gives up.

"The average cost for IVF, including medications, is around fifteen to twenty thousand per cycle," Dr. Rowland says. "Some patients need multiple cycles."

I do the math automatically—a skill honed by twenty years in business consulting. My savings account—or the account I've allotted to this decision, no need to touch my retirement accounts—has forty-three thousand. Enough for two cycles, maybe three if I'm careful. If I don't get pregnant within three tries, I'm done. Game over.

"I want to start with IUI," I hear myself say. "Three cycles. If that doesn't work, we reassess."

Dr. Rowland nods, types notes into her computer. "That's a reasonable approach. We'll need to track your cycle, determine ovulation timing—"

My phone buzzes in my purse. Once, twice, insistent. I ignore it.

"—and we'll start with the least invasive interventions first," Dr. Rowland continues. "I have to ask, do you have support at home? Family, friends? This process can be emotionally taxing, and having people you can lean on makes a significant difference."

Support. I think of my mother in Portland who lives in a 55+ resort-style community (where half of my savings went to get her settled five months ago), who still asks when I'm going to "settle down properly" and has already told me forty-one is too old for first-time motherhood. I think of my small circle of friends, most of them with kids already, busy with soccer practices and school pickups. I think of Lauren Donovan, my best friend, who'll be there no matter what but has her own life.

"I have enough," I say.

Dr. Rowland's pen pauses for half a second before she continues writing. "The first step is scheduling your baseline appointment. We'll do that on day three of your next cycle, and if everything looks good, we'll proceed with your first IUI attempt."

We schedule appointments. She hands me pamphlets with titles like "Single Motherhood by Choice" and "Your Fertility Journey" that I'll probably never read. We shake hands. She wishes me luck.

I walk back through the lavender-scented waiting room, past the couple still holding hands, past the reception desk with its inspirational quotes about miracles and hope.

Outside, San Francisco unfolds in its typical fall glory—crisp air, brilliant sky, the city bustling with people rushing to meetings, grabbing coffee, living their lives.

I pull out my phone. Three missed calls from a number I don't recognize. Two voicemails. One email from Angela Nolan, a headhunter I've worked with before.

Subject: High-Priority Opportunity - Pierce Enterprises

I almost delete it. I'm done with corporate consulting. Done with eighteen-hour days and impossible clients and sacrificing my personal life for someone else's crisis. That's what got me here in the first place—forty-one years old, single, starting over.

But something makes me open it.

Cassie,

I know you're taking time for yourself, but this opportunity is too good not to pass along. Pierce Enterprises needs a compliance officer immediately—six-month contract, full operational authority, compensation package that I think will interest you considerably. They specifically asked if you were available.

The company recently went through a significant transition, and they need someone with your expertise to stabilize operations and restore investor confidence. The CEO is young but impressive—Stanford MBA, strong track record. I think you'd work well together.

Call me if you want details. The compensation alone is worth a conversation.

Best, Angela

I stand on the sidewalk, people flowing around me, and stare at the email.

Six months. That's manageable. And if the compensation is as good as Angela implies, it might be enough to cover multiple IVF cycles if the IUI fails. It might be enough to give me options, security, breathing room.

I hate that I'm even considering it.

Six years ago, I would have jumped at an opportunity like this. I was engaged to Brad, building my reputation as one of the top operational consultants in the Bay Area, taking every high-profile client, saying yes to everything because I believed hard work and sacrifice would pay off eventually.

Then I came home early from a conference in Seattle—my keynote got canceled—and found Brad in our bed with someone else. His assistant. The one he'd hired six months earlier, the one he said I was being "paranoid" about when I asked why she texted him at midnight.

I packed a bag that night. Ended the engagement by email the next morning because I couldn't stand to hear his voice. Spent the next three months finding a new apartment, a new therapist, and a new understanding of how thoroughly I'd ignored every red flag because I was too busy working.

Eight months, it turned out. He'd been sleeping with her for eight months while I worked late on client presentations and missed dinners and believed him when he said my career was "intimidating."

I made a decision after that: no more sacrificing what I want for men who can't handle my success. No more waiting for the perfect situation. No more someday.

If I want a baby, I'll have a baby. If I want a family, I'll create one. On my terms.

Except terms require resources. And resources require money.

I pull up my banking app, look at the number that felt substantial a month ago and now feels frighteningly finite. Then I look at Dr. Rowland's estimate again. Fifteen to twenty thousand per IVF cycle.

My phone rings. Angela.

"Tell me you're at least curious," she says without preamble.

"I'm trying not to be."

"The base salary is three hundred thousand for six months. Performance bonus of two hundred thousand if you hit stabilization targets, which, knowing you, you will."

Half a million dollars. For six months of work.

That's three, maybe four IVF cycles. That's security. That's options.

That's also eighteen-hour days, impossible expectations, corporate politics, and sacrificing the personal life I'm trying to build.

"Cassie, the offer won't stay on the table forever. Think of it as a temporary career boost while you're figuring out your next move."

It's a valid point. And if anyone knows me, it's Angela. She's watched me come back from every challenge—from breakups to client disasters, from the time a client's project collapsed and I had to scramble to salvage a quarter-million-dollar contract. She's never seen me turn down an opportunity.

"Can you get me the proposal?" I hear myself ask. "Send me the terms, the contract. Let's see if it's a good fit."

I hang up and stand there, feeling the rush of the city around me. The email was a surprise. But now that it's sunk in, I can't help thinking: Maybe this is the universe's way of giving me the resources to make a choice. Maybe this is my chance to prove I'm still capable of thriving, even with all the changes in my life.

Or maybe this is just a six-month gig that gets me enough money to keep trying.

Either way, I'll fight for the right to be a mother. To have the family I've wanted. And if that means going back to the corporate world, so be it.

My phone buzzes with a message from Lauren, inviting me to a girls' night tonight. She knows I'm stressed. Knows I've been looking into fertility treatments. She's always there, supporting me.

I text her back, letting her know I'll be there.

Maybe some wine and laughter will help me forget the choices looming ahead.

Because even though this opportunity sounds like a dream, there's a lot to lose.

My friends. My peace of mind. My sanity.

The job's also in Los Angeles, which means I have to live

there for the next six months. No more weekend trips to the beach. No more casual coffee dates with Lauren. No more evenings at the art gallery where she exhibits her photography.

I'm not saying no, but I'm not saying yes, either. Not yet.

I pull up my phone and look up Pierce Enterprises. Why does the name sound familiar? As the results pop up on my screen, suddenly I remember. Seven months ago, their CEO stepped down abruptly, Declan Pierce, the late Maxwell Pierce's son. He took over after his father died of a heart attack while surveying a future commercial property, and for five years, he ran Pierce Enterprises.

Then came a protest from Highland Community Center, practically a twenty-year-old Los Angeles institution that they had recently evicted (or tried to) with demolition scheduled without any relocation assistance offered.

The news had sparked a backlash, with residents and local businesses banding together to stop the eviction. They rallied. They protested. They fought for their neighborhood, their heritage.

Somewhere along the way, something happened to make the CEO step down. And now they need someone to oversee operations.

I scroll through the website. Pierce Enterprises has offices in Los Angeles, San Francisco, and Seattle. They invest in a variety of real estate ventures—everything from condos to shopping centers.

My finger hovers over the link for the executive management. But before I can tap the link, my phone buzzes with a message from Angela, the attached PDF showing me exactly what's on the table.

"Come on," I tell myself as I open the document and read

the specifics. "You've never walked away from an opportunity before."

That's not entirely true. There have been plenty of opportunities I've walked away from. But that's always been personal. This is business.

Half a million dollars for six months' worth of work. More than enough to try to have a a baby and maybe even take a year or two off to be a stay-at-home mother.

Which means having a baby can wait.

I pause.

Having a baby can wait.

How many times have I told myself that over the years? When I was building my career at Coe Compliance Group. When I made partner. When Brad and I were together and I kept pushing it off because the timing was never quite right.

And now I'm doing it again. Postponing. Delaying. Choosing career over the thing I actually want.

Except this time it's different. This time I have an end date. Six months. Then I'm done, back to San Francisco, ready to start the fertility treatments with enough money saved to do it right.

It's strategic, not avoidance.

At least that's what I tell myself as I pull up Dr. Rowland's number to reschedule my procedure.

Career now, family later. Both things, just not simultaneously.

I take a deep breath. I can live with that.

2

Elliot

"...AND THAT'S THE OVERVIEW," Melinda Finnegan says, closing her folder with a decisive snap.

The board meeting has already gone twenty minutes over, which means I'm already behind on a day that started at five-thirty when my flight arrived from Portland. I have back-to-back meetings until six, a conference call with the Portland office at seven, and somewhere in there I need to eat actual food instead of surviving on coffee and whatever Chief Financial Officer Colton Parker left in the executive kitchen.

"Any questions before we adjourn?" Melinda asks, her tone suggesting she's hoping the answer is no.

"Just one observation."

Of course. Harrison Gordon always has one observation.

He leans back in his chair at the opposite end of the conference table, sixty-two years old and radiating the particular brand of smug condescension that comes from being passed over for CEO. Twice. First when founder Maxwell Pierce died and the board chose his son Declan over Harrison. Then seven months ago when Declan stepped down and the board chose me instead.

Harrison hasn't forgiven either slight. And he makes sure I know it at every possible opportunity.

"And what is that, Harrison?" Melinda's tone is patient, but I can hear the edge underneath. She's dealt with him longer than I have, knows his patterns better than anyone.

"I want assurance that this leadership—" He pauses deliberately, glances in my direction with barely concealed disdain. "—won't be as distracted as the previous administration. We can't afford another situation like the Anderson Project."

Around the table, board members shift uncomfortably. Douglas Baker's jaw tightens. Patricia Morris looks annoyed.

My own jaw tightens but I keep my expression carefully neutral. Harrison wants a reaction. Wants me to get defensive, to stumble, to show some crack in my composure he can exploit.

I won't give him the satisfaction.

The Anderson Project. The disaster that led to Declan's resignation seven months ago. Harrison had pushed through a plan to demolish a downtown LA city block to build luxury condos, completely ignoring exit protocols for Highland Community Center—a twenty-year-old institution serving hundreds of families in the area.

When Maya Navarro—daughter of the center's late founder—confronted us about it, Declan investigated and discovered that Harrison had deliberately ignored established protocols because he didn't think the Navarro family deserved the courtesy.

Turns out, he and Maxwell Pierce had tried to buy that property a decade earlier, failed, and when Pierce Enterprises finally managed to buy it last year, Harrison saw the demolition as his chance to settle an old score. He'd bypassed the proper notification channels entirely, hoping the center would simply disappear without the Navarros having any say in the matter.

Declan tried to make it right. Bought the property himself, put it in a land trust to protect the community center. Saved the organization but it cost him his position as CEO because the board saw it as too personal, too emotional, evidence that his relationship with Maya had compromised his judgment.

Never mind that Harrison was the one who created the disaster in the first place. But Harrison had seniority, decades of successful deals, and enough allies on the board to spin the narrative his way. While Declan got painted as the emotional young CEO who let personal relationships cloud his business judgment, Harrison positioned himself as the seasoned executive who'd simply made a "procedural oversight." The fact that his "oversight" was deliberate sabotage got buried under his track record and his carefully cultivated reputation as Pierce Enterprises' most reliable rainmaker.

And now Harrison wants to rewrite history. Wants to pretend Declan was the problem, that young CEOs are too emotional, too easily distracted. Wants to plant seeds of doubt about whether I'll make the same mistakes.

"The Anderson Project was resolved," I say, keeping my voice level but firm. "Pierce Enterprises recovered from that debacle. Our stock price is up eighteen percent year-over-year. We've closed three major deals in the last quarter alone. What the situation revealed was a failure of protocol enforcement—which is why we've since implemented additional oversight on all development projects. The company is stronger now because we learned from it."

It's a careful answer. Acknowledges the problem without throwing Declan under the bus. Points to systemic solutions and concrete business results without directly blaming Harrison, even though everyone in this room knows he was responsible.

"Because you've implemented oversight," he says, leaning forward now with the expression of someone who thinks they're about to make a winning argument, "or because you won't let personal relationships cloud your judgment the way Declan did?"

Around the table, board members react. Douglas shifts uncomfortably. Patricia's expression tightens with poorly concealed irritation. Melinda's watching me carefully, waiting to see how I handle this.

This is a test. Not just from Harrison—from all of them. They need to know I can handle political attacks without losing my composure.

"The oversight exists precisely because someone—" I look directly at Harrison, hold his gaze without blinking, "—ignored established protocols. That someone wasn't Declan. And the board is well aware of who was responsible for that failure. What matters now is that Pierce Enterprises has implemented systems to prevent it from happening again, and our results speak for themselves."

I say it calmly. Factually. No heat, no anger. Just truth delivered with the kind of professional courtesy that makes it impossible for him to claim I'm being hostile.

Red creeps up Harrison's neck. His jaw works like he's physically restraining himself from saying what he really wants to say. For a second, I think he's going to lose his composure—really lose it, say something that crosses a line.

Then Douglas clears his throat, breaking the tension.

"I think we've covered this ground sufficiently," Douglas says, his tone diplomatic but final. He's been one of my strongest supporters on the board, and right now I'm grateful for it. "The Anderson Project situation has been addressed. Pierce Enterprises has stronger protocols in place and our financial performance demonstrates effective leadership. Unless there are current performance concerns about Elliot's leadership, I suggest we move on."

"I'm simply saying we should be vigilant," Harrison says, but there's frustration in his voice now. He wanted me to get defensive, to stumble, to give him ammunition. I didn't. "Personal entanglements, romantic distractions—they compromise judgment. The board has a responsibility to ensure that doesn't happen again."

"Noted," Melinda says with finality, making it clear the discussion is over. "Now, before we adjourn, I need to inform everyone of a decision the board made last week."

She pulls out a different folder. "As you know, when Declan stepped down, the company underwent significant restructuring. The board appointed Elliot as interim CEO with a six-month evaluation period. That period has concluded successfully—" She nods toward me. "—which is why we've now confirmed Elliot's permanent appointment as CEO of Pierce Enterprises."

There are murmurs of approval around the table. Douglas smiles. Patricia nods. Even Harrison manages a tight-lipped acknowledgment.

"However," Melinda continues, "given the compliance failures that led to the Anderson Project situation, the board has also created a new position: Chief Compliance Officer. This was a unanimous decision—" She glances meaningfully at Harrison, and I understand immediately that he pushed for this, probably thinking it would create oversight that limits my authority. "—to ensure we have the proper checks and balances in place going forward."

My jaw tightens slightly. A Chief Compliance Officer. Reporting directly to the board. Someone who'll be watching every decision I make, every protocol I follow, ready to flag anything that looks remotely like the kind of "personal compromise" Harrison just warned about.

"We completed the search last week," Melinda continues. "Six-month contract initially, with the possibility of permanent placement. The position includes direct board reporting for compliance matters, operational audit authority, and collaborative oversight with our CEO on all major initiatives."

She pauses, and I realize she's looking directly at me now.

"I'm pleased to announce that Cassandra Reynolds has accepted our offer and starts today."

I'm exhausted enough that the name takes a second to register.

Then it hits me.

Cassandra Reynolds.

My coffee cup stops halfway to my mouth.

"I'm sorry," I say, setting down the cup carefully, keeping my voice steady even though my heart just lurched. "Could you repeat that name?"

"Cassandra Reynolds," Melinda repeats, pulling up something on her tablet. "Coe Compliance Group partner, extensive operational compliance background, excellent references. She'll be reporting directly to the board with authority to audit any department."

Cassandra Reynolds. Cassie. My Stanford mentor. The woman who spent a full year teaching me how to think strategically, how to lead, how to question assumptions.

She's here. The board hired her while I was in Portland putting out fires.

"You look surprised," Douglas says, watching me carefully. "Is there a problem?"

"No, I—" I clear my throat, trying to find my professional voice. "Cassandra Reynolds. If this is the same person, she was my business strategy mentor at Stanford. Seven years ago."

The reaction around the table is more subdued than I expected. A few nods of recognition, but no surprise.

"Yes, we're aware of the Stanford connection," Melinda says calmly. "It came up during the vetting process."

My eyes cut to Harrison, wondering if he raised objections during hiring. But his expression is unreadable—just that slight tightness around his mouth that means he's filed this information away for future use.

"And the committee determined it wasn't a conflict?" I ask, trying to sound professionally curious rather than concerned.

"It was discussed," Douglas says. "But the mentorship ended seven years ago, and the relationship was purely professional. We didn't see it as an issue—if anything, her familiarity with your strategic thinking could be valuable for the assessment."

"Ms. Reynolds' credentials are impeccable," Melinda adds. "Twenty years of compliance work, specializing in tech and finance sectors. Multiple successful engagements with companies similar in size and complexity to Pierce. The Stanford connection was noted but not considered disqualifying."

I can feel Harrison's gaze on me, assessing my reaction. Looking for any sign that this bothers me more than it should.

"I agree it's not an issue," I say firmly, projecting confidence I don't entirely feel. "She's excellent at what she does —strategic, thorough, completely objective. I'm confident she'll provide valuable insights."

It's not entirely true. Yes, she was excellent. But I'm leaving out the part about the crush I had for her. The completely inappropriate feelings I told myself were just admiration for someone brilliant. The moment at graduation when I stupidly asked her to coffee and she gently shut me down because she was engaged.

But no one around this table needs to know any of that.

"Good," Melinda says, seeming satisfied with my response. "Ms. Reynolds will have full access to operational data, personnel files, board meeting minutes—everything she needs to conduct a comprehensive assessment. We expect complete transparency and cooperation from leadership."

"Of course." I keep my voice steady, professional. "When does she start?"

"Today. She should be arriving around nine for orientation." Melinda glances at her watch. "Actually, she's probably already here. Jennifer from HR was handling badge pickup and initial paperwork."

Today. She's here today. Probably in the building right now, getting her badge made and filling out forms. My heart is racing. I force myself to breathe normally, to keep my expression neutral.

"I'd like to meet with her this morning," I say, managing to sound calm and professional. "Get aligned on how we'll work together, clarify reporting structures, make sure she has everything she needs."

"Good idea," Melinda says approvingly. "I'll have Jennifer let her know you'll stop by her office once she's settled."

"If there's nothing else," Melinda says, "we're adjourned. Elliot, a word before you go?"

The other board members file out. Harrison lingers for a moment, making a show of gathering his papers slowly. He's hoping to overhear whatever Melinda wants to discuss privately.

"That includes you, Harrison," Melinda says pointedly.

He leaves, but not before giving me one last look that says *I'm watching this situation very carefully.*

When we're alone, Melinda turns to me with an expression that's part concern, part assessment.

"Be honest with me," she says quietly. "Is the prior relationship with Ms. Reynolds going to be a problem?"

"No," I say, and I mean it. "We had a good professional relationship at Stanford. She was an excellent mentor. That was seven years ago."

"Good. Because Harrison was actually the one who pushed hardest for her hiring." She sees my surprise and nods. "He reviewed her credentials personally, noted the Stanford connection, and told the committee it wouldn't be an issue. Said having someone who understood your strategic thinking would make the assessment more thorough."

I go very still. "Harrison advocated for hiring my former mentor?"

"Enthusiastically. Which should tell you something about his motives." Melinda's expression is knowing. "He's not worried about the connection being a problem. He's counting on it being one."

The realization settles in my stomach like lead. Harrison isn't concerned about a conflict of interest—he's hoping for it. He wants Cassie to either find problems with my leadership or have our prior relationship complicate her objectivity. Either outcome gives him ammunition.

"So this is a trap," I say flatly.

"It's Harrison being strategic. He knows if Ms. Reynolds finds legitimate issues, it reflects poorly on you. And if her assessment appears too favorable, he can question whether the Stanford connection compromised her independence." Melinda's tone is matter-of-fact. "He wins either way— unless you and Ms. Reynolds both do impeccable work that gives him nothing to exploit."

"No pressure."

"You wanted this position. This is what it looks like." But her expression softens slightly. "For what it's worth, I think you can handle it. And I think Ms. Reynolds will be excellent for this company. Her record is impeccable, personal break notwithstanding. Just keep everything professional and documented. Don't give Harrison any ammunition."

"I won't."

"Good." She picks up her folder, heading for the door. Then pauses. "And Elliot? Harrison's going to watch this situation very carefully. If there's anything beyond a professional connection—anything at all that could complicate this arrangement—now would be the time to tell me."

"There's nothing," I say firmly. "It was a professional mentoring relationship seven years ago. That's all."

She holds my gaze for a long moment, then nods. "Then you have nothing to worry about. Just do excellent work and let the results speak for themselves."

After she leaves, I sit alone in the conference room, trying to process what just happened.

Cassie Reynolds is here. In this building. Starting today as Chief Compliance Officer.

She's been hired specifically to audit my decisions. To monitor my leadership. To report to the board about whether I'm making sound judgments or letting personal considerations cloud my thinking.

I can do this.

I have to do this.

Because the alternative is giving Harrison exactly the ammunition he's looking for.

3

Cassie

I CAN'T BELIEVE it's been two weeks since I first was considered for the position but here I am at Pierce Enterprises on my first day unpacking the last box of compliance books in my new office. Six months. Excellent pay. And then I can proceed with my plan to be a mother.

I'm about to shelve the last stack of frameworks when there's a knock on my door.

"Come in," I say, setting down the books.

The door opens and Elliot Walker walks into my office.

"Elliot," I say, extending my hand. "It's good to see you."

"Cassie." He steps inside, closes the door behind him with a quiet click. "I have to admit, when Melinda said Cassandra Reynolds this morning, I didn't—I mean, I did, but I couldn't quite believe it."

"You didn't know I was the candidate?" I'm genuinely surprised. "The board didn't tell you?"

"They hired you while I was in Portland last week dealing with a crisis. I found out in this morning's board meeting when Melinda announced you were starting today."

He runs a hand through his hair—a gesture I remember from Stanford when he was working through a difficult problem. "So I've had about three hours to process the fact that my Stanford mentor is now Pierce's Chief Compliance Officer."

I chuckle. "And here I've had a week to process that my former student is now the CEO I'll be monitoring." I gesture to the chair across from my desk. "Should we sit? This feels like a conversation that requires sitting."

A slight smile crosses his face—brief but genuine. "Probably a good idea."

As he takes a seat across from my desk, I can't help but notice how much he's changed in the seven years that have gone by. He's thirty-two now—no longer the twenty-five-year-old who used to sit in my office hours arguing about case studies with that mix of brilliance and arrogance that made him simultaneously my best student and my most challenging one.

He's filled out slightly. Broader shoulders, more presence. The sharp suit is perfectly tailored—charcoal gray, crisp white shirt, navy tie. His dark hair is shorter than I remember, professionally styled. There's a confidence in the way he carries himself that wasn't there before, the kind that comes from years of proving himself and succeeding.

He looks like a CEO.

"So," I start, folding my hands on my desk. "I'm guessing you have questions."

"Several." He leans back in his chair. "Starting with: You knew I was the CEO when you accepted the position?"

"I knew you were the interim CEO during the interview process," I clarify. "Your permanent appointment wasn't confirmed until last week."

His eyebrow lifts slightly. "And our history?"

"I disclosed it to Melinda and the search committee during my final interview." I meet his gaze directly. "I told them we had a mentor-student relationship at Stanford seven years ago, that it was professional and academic in nature, and that I didn't believe it would compromise my ability to provide independent oversight."

"What did they say?"

"Harrison Gordon was the one who responded." I keep my voice neutral, but I remember the moment clearly. Harrison had leaned back in his chair, waving a dismissive hand. "He said—and I'm quoting—'Seven years ago, different context, purely academic. If we disqualified every compliance officer who'd ever worked with someone they knew professionally, we'd never fill the position. Non-issue.'"

Elliot's expression shifts. Something wary flickers across his face. "Harrison said that."

It's not a question. It's something else—concern, maybe, or calculation. Like he's processing information I can't see.

"He did," I say carefully, watching his reaction. "Melinda and Douglas agreed. They seemed satisfied that the relationship was distant enough and professional enough not to constitute a conflict." I pause. "Should I be concerned that Harrison was so quick to dismiss it?"

"No." The answer comes too fast, too smooth. Professional deflection. "Harrison and I have... different operational styles. He tends to be more focused on bottom-line results, while I prioritize sustainable systems and long-term thinking. It creates friction sometimes."

It's a diplomatic answer. The kind a CEO gives when he doesn't want to badmouth a board member to someone he just reconnected with. But the careful phrasing tells me there's more to the story.

"Different operational styles," I repeat, keeping my tone neutral. "That's one way to put it."

His mouth quirks slightly—almost a smile, but not quite. "Let's just say Harrison has very strong opinions about how Pierce should be run, and he's not always supportive when my decisions don't align with his preferences."

"And hiring me—someone with a prior professional connection to you—that doesn't concern you?"

"Should it?" He leans back slightly, and I can see him choosing his words with care. "You're here to provide independent compliance oversight. If you do your job well—and I have no doubt you will—then it shouldn't matter what our history is. The work speaks for itself."

It's a reasonable answer. A confident answer. The kind of answer a CEO gives when he wants to project certainty.

But I catch the slight tension in his shoulders. The way his hand tightens almost imperceptibly on the arm of his chair when I mentioned Harrison's name.

There's something he's not saying. Something about Harrison that makes him wary, but I file it away. Part of compliance work is understanding the politics beneath the surface, reading what people don't say as much as what they do say.

"Fair enough," I say. "Then I'll make sure my work speaks very clearly." I stand up, needing to move, to shift the energy in this room. "I should probably see the rest of the executive floor. Get oriented, understand how operations actually flow here versus what's in the org charts."

"Good idea." He stands, too, moving toward the door, then pauses. "Fair warning: it's chaos today. We've got three major deals closing this week, the acquisition team is under-water, and half the executive team is in New York for merger negotiations."

"Perfect," I say, and I mean it. "I'd rather see how things work under pressure than during a calm week."

He leads me out of my office, and immediately I'm struck by the energy of the floor. People are moving with purpose—quick conversations in doorways, someone rushing past with an armful of presentation boards, the distant sound of raised voices from what must be a conference room.

"That's Colton Parker's office," Elliot says, gesturing to a corner space where I can see someone on a video call, gesturing emphatically at his screen. "CFO. He's been here since six this morning working on the Blaisdell merger numbers. If you need financial data for compliance reviews, he's your guy—but bring coffee as tribute."

I make a mental note. "Noted."

We pass a glass-walled conference room where several people are in what looks like an intense strategy session. Elliot doesn't slow down, but I catch him glancing in, his expression tightening slightly.

"Problem?" I ask.

"Development team. They're presenting a new property acquisition proposal this afternoon, and I can already tell from here that they haven't done the community impact assessment I requested." He keeps walking. "Which is exactly the kind of thing you'll be catching going forward."

There's no resentment in his voice when he says it. Just matter-of-fact acknowledgment that oversight is needed.

We turn a corner, and suddenly the atmosphere shifts. Quieter here. More traditional. Executive row.

"Harrison's office," Elliot says, nodding toward a closed

door with dark wood and frosted glass. "He's rarely here—spends most of his time at our New York office. But when he is here, he tends to... make his presence known."

I file that away too. Understanding office dynamics is crucial for compliance work. You need to know where the power actually sits versus where the org chart says it sits.

Elliot shows me the executive conference room—sleek, modern, clearly designed to intimidate—and then leads me toward a more casual space. Open layout, comfortable seating, a coffee station that looks better stocked than most cafés.

"This is where the real work happens," he says, and there's warmth in his voice now. "Formal meetings happen in the conference room. But actual problem-solving? Decision-making? That happens here, usually around ten PM when everyone's too tired to maintain professional distance."

I can picture it. The exhausted honesty of late-night work sessions. The kind of conversations where people say what they actually think instead of what they're supposed to think.

"You'll probably spend time here too," Elliot continues. "Compliance isn't just about auditing paperwork. It's about understanding how decisions really get made."

He's right, and the fact that he knows that tells me something important about how he thinks about leadership.

We're walking back toward my office when my phone buzzes. I glance at it—a reminder I set weeks ago, before I accepted this position, back when my timeline was still straightforward.

Dr. Martinez initial consultation - 2 weeks. Confirm appointment.

Two weeks until my first real appointment at the fertility clinic. Two weeks to finalize the decision I've been planning for six months. The informational consultation months ago laid out my options—IUI, IVF, the statistics, the costs, the realities. But this appointment is different. This is where I commit. Where I choose a donor, establish my baseline fertility assessment, map out the actual timeline.

I silence the reminder, but the weight of it sits heavy in my chest.

Two weeks until I formally start the process of becoming a mother. Six months to prove I can still operate at the highest level of my profession.

And Harrison Gordon waiting in the wings to use my past connection with Elliot against one or both of us the moment it becomes convenient.

I disclosed that relationship in good faith. I was honest about the history, transparent about the nature of it, clear about my ability to remain objective. And Harrison dismissed it as irrelevant—not because he genuinely believed it was irrelevant, but because it served his purposes to let me walk into this role with that connection hanging between Elliot and me like a loaded gun he could fire whenever he wanted.

I should have seen it. Should have recognized the trap.

But I was focused on the opportunity, the timeline, the chance to do meaningful work before stepping away for motherhood. I trusted that if the board deemed it acceptable, it was acceptable.

Now I know better.

"You good?" Elliot's voice breaks through my thoughts.

I realize I've stopped walking. We're back at my office door, and he's watching me with that same focused attention from earlier.

"Fine," I say, pulling myself back to the present. "Just processing. It's a lot to take in."

"It is." He leans against the doorframe, and something in his posture relaxes slightly. Less CEO, more... human. "Look, I know this situation is complicated. The history, the roles, all of it. But I want you to know—I'm glad you're here. Genuinely. This company needs what you do, and from what I remember, you're exceptionally good at it."

The compliment lands unexpectedly. I'm not used to executives being openly appreciative of compliance work. Usually they tolerate it at best.

"Thank you," I say. "That means something."

"I mean it. And Cassie—" He pauses, seeming to weigh his words. "If at any point this becomes untenable, if the history makes it impossible to work together effectively, just tell me. We'll figure out a solution. I don't want you feeling trapped in a situation that doesn't work."

It's a generous offer. More generous than I expected.

"I appreciate that. But I don't anticipate any problems." I meet his eyes. "I'm here to do a job. Six months, focused work, implement better systems. That's it."

"Six months?" His eyebrow lifts slightly. "The contract mentioned the possibility of permanent placement."

"I know. But I have personal plans after the six months. The timing works for what I need."

I don't elaborate. He doesn't ask.

"Understood," he says simply. Then, after a beat: "Well then. Let's make it a productive six months."

He pushes off the doorframe, already turning back

toward his office, his mind clearly moving to the next thing on his endless list.

"Elliot," I call after him as he turns back to look at me. "For what it's worth, I'm glad I'm here too."

His smile is brief but genuine. "Good. Now go make us better at following our own rules."

And then he's gone, disappearing into his office, leaving me standing in my doorway with the weight of two timelines pressing against each other.

Six months to prove I can still do this work at the highest level. Two weeks until I take the first formal step toward becoming a mother.

Both true. Both necessary. Both terrifying in completely different ways.

I step into my office and close the door.

Time to get to work.

4

Elliot

Highland Community Center is still open when I arrive at seven. The building looks different than it did seven months ago—better maintained, with fresh paint on the exterior, new windows, a rooftop garden that catches the evening light. The kind of renovations that signal investment and care rather than the demolition that Harrison had planned.

Declan's car is in the parking lot. Maya's, too. They're probably still here wrapping up after the after-school programs.

I used to come here every week after Declan walked away from Pierce Enterprises, mainly to make sure he was okay. We'd talk business—transition issues, board politics, operational questions, his plans after Pierce—but those conversations tapered off months ago as I found my footing as CEO. Now I come for different reasons.

The community center reminds me of something I've spent years trying to forget, or at least set aside: my mother's world. The one she tried to share with me and my sisters since we were children, before I decided that succeeding in my father's world—the world of Pierce Enterprises and LA power players—meant leaving hers behind.

She was from Manila, came to the States for grad school and never left. Married my father, who was white and wealthy and very certain about how things should be done. She tried to teach me Tagalog, took me to Filipino community events, cooked food that my father politely tolerated but never really understood.

I look like him. Always have. Light skin, Western features, the kind of appearance that lets me move through corporate America without anyone questioning whether I belong. My mother used to joke that I got my father's face but her stubborn streak, her capacity for loyalty.

But I let that part of myself fade. Not intentionally, not with any dramatic rejection—just gradually, as I focused on business school, on proving myself at Pierce, on becoming the kind of executive my father's world would respect. It was easier to be just Elliot Walker, the CEO, rather than Elliot Walker who was half-Filipino but didn't look it and wasn't sure how to claim that identity anyway.

Highland changed that calculation. The center serves a heavily Filipino community—families like the one my mother came from, the world she wanted me to understand. Being here, watching Maya run programs my mother would have loved, hearing Tagalog in the hallways... it surfaces things I thought I'd successfully compartmentalized.

Declan doesn't know most of this. Neither does Maya, really. But they've noticed that I keep coming back even when there's no business reason to be here, that I linger during community events, that I ask questions about the programs and the families they serve.

Maybe that's why I'm here tonight, hours after I should

have gone home to my empty house in Eagle Rock. Because Highland feels like something real in a way that most of my life doesn't. And because talking to Declan about it—about anything beyond Pierce's quarterly projections—feels like reconnecting with a version of myself I abandoned too quickly.

I park and head inside, following the sound of voices and activity toward the main community room.

The space is transformed from when I last saw it. New flooring, updated lighting, colorful murals on the walls depicting Filipino heritage and community scenes. Kids' artwork is displayed on bulletin boards. There's a new computer lab visible through glass doors—the one Maya got funded through some tech company grant.

Declan's in the community room moving chairs back into place while Maya's collecting art supplies from what looks like a craft session. They're talking and laughing about something, that easy rhythm of people who've been together long enough that even cleanup feels companionable.

"Knock knock," I call out from the doorway.

They both turn. Declan breaks into a grin. "Walk! What brings you here?"

"Thought I'd see what you've done with the place since I was last here," I say, stepping through the door. "How's the computer lab?"

"It's incredible," Maya says, setting down the box of markers she was collecting. "Twelve new computers, software for coding classes, even a 3D printer. The kids are obsessed."

"That's great. You should be proud of what you've built here."

"We're getting there." Declan moves another few chairs.

"Hey, you want to help with cleanup and then stay for a sungka game? We were about to play a round before heading home."

I grin. "Yeah, I'd like that."

We finish the cleanup quickly—chairs stacked, art supplies organized, floors swept. Maya brings out the sungka board from a cabinet, the wooden game worn smooth from use. It's beautiful—traditional carved wood with shells for playing pieces, the kind my mother kept on a shelf in our living room.

The boat-shaped board has two rows of seven small holes and two larger holes at each end—the "head" where you collect your pieces. Each small hole starts with seven shells. The goal is to capture more shells than your opponent by strategically moving them around the board.

"Okay, so remind me how this works," Declan says as we settle around the table.

Maya picks up shells from one of her holes. "You pick up all the shells from one of your holes and distribute them one by one into the next holes, moving counterclockwise. If your last shell lands in your head, you get another turn. If it lands in an empty hole on your side and there are shells in the hole directly across from it, you capture those shells plus the one you just placed."

"And you're trying to get the most shells in your head by the end," I add.

"Right." Maya looks at Declan. "It's about planning several moves ahead. You want to set yourself up for captures while blocking your opponent's opportunities."

"Thoughtful strategy," I say. "Not random shell distribution."

Declan sighs. "One time I said my strategy was 'intuitive' and now I never hear the end of it."

We start playing, with Maya playing against me while Declan watches. Whoever loses forfeits the next game. Maya's good—precise, calculating, always thinking two or three moves ahead. I'm rusty but the patterns come back quickly, muscle memory from countless games with my mother and sisters around the kitchen table.

When Maya loses to me, Declan takes her place while she tries to coach him.

"This game is rigged," he announces after I capture another cluster of his shells.

"The game is fine. Your strategy needs work," Maya says, but she's laughing.

"Strategy? You're supposed to be coaching me," he says as we set up the board again, this time with Maya taking Declan's position.

As we play the next round, conversation flows easily—Maya talking about new programming ideas for the center, Declan mentioning a business opportunity he's considering, me offering occasional thoughts but mostly just enjoying being here, being part of something that isn't Pierce Enterprises or board politics or Harrison's constant undermining.

This feels like something my mother would have understood. Community. Connection. The kind of belonging that doesn't require proving yourself worthy of it.

Maya's phone buzzes. She checks it and makes a face.

"Tita Rosa's calling—she probably wants to talk about the fundraiser next month. I should take this." She stands, squeezes Declan's shoulder. "You take my place. I'll be back."

She heads toward the office, phone already to her ear.

Declan and I continue the game in comfortable silence

for a minute before he says, "So, what's really going on? You don't usually stop by on a Monday evening unless something's on your mind."

"The board hired a Chief Compliance Officer while I was in Portland last week."

Declan nods, his expression thoughtful. "Makes sense after what happened with the Anderson Project."

"It's Cassie Reynolds."

His hand pauses mid-move. He looks up. "*Your* Cassie Reynolds? Stanford mentor Cassie Reynolds?"

"The same," I reply, "But she's not exactly mine."

"Holy shit." He sits back, abandoning the game entirely. "Holy shit indeed."

He's grinning now. "Walk, this is huge. How did you not lead with this?"

"Because it's not huge. It's just... unexpected." I move a few shells absently.

"Did you know they were considering her?"

"No idea. They kept the search tight—just Melinda and a few others, including Harrison," I reply, "Didn't involve me, which makes sense. The whole point is independent oversight."

"But of all people." Declan's still grinning. "Cassie Reynolds. The woman you spent a full year being quietly obsessed with."

I can feel my face burning. "I wasn't obsessed."

"You talked about her constantly. Every mentorship session, you'd come back energized, talking about whatever insight she'd shared or question she'd challenged you with," he says, chuckling. "You had it bad."

I did, and that's the uncomfortable truth. For a full year at Stanford, Cassie Reynolds was the most compelling person in my orbit. Brilliant, challenging, funny in this dry way that always caught me off guard. She was thirty-three to my twenty-four, already successful, completely out of my league.

And she saw me as a student. A promising one, maybe, but still just a kid learning how to think strategically.

"That was seven years ago," I say. "A lot has changed since then."

"Like what?"

"Like I grew up. Had actual relationships with women who weren't my mentor," I reply, wondering why I'm suddenly feeling defensive. "Cecilia, for two years—"

"Until she wanted commitment and you bailed."

"I didn't bail. We wanted different things." It's a defensive response and we both know it. "Oh, there was Amanda for eight months, and before that, a few shorter ones. So if you're implying I've been pining over my former mentor, you're wrong."

"How did it feel seeing her again?"

I think about this morning. Seeing Cassie in her office looking exactly like I remembered but also completely different. More self-possessed. More confident.

Beautiful.

"Strange," I admit. "She's more... settled into herself, if that makes sense. Like she knows exactly who she is and doesn't need anyone's approval."

Declan's watching me with that analytical expression that means he's reading between the lines. "You're still attracted to her."

"I'm *aware* of her," I say carefully. "Aware that she's impressive and compelling and that working with her is going to require very careful boundary management."

He arches an eyebrow. "Because?"

"Because she's the compliance officer monitoring my leadership. Because Harrison's watching for any excuse to question my judgment. And because getting involved with her would be catastrophically stupid." I pause. "She's here to do a job, nothing more. Six months, then she's gone. She has personal plans that don't include staying at Pierce."

"What kind of personal plans?"

"She didn't say," I reply, "But she was definitive about the timeline."

"Is she married?"

The question catches me slightly off guard. "I didn't notice a ring."

"At least you checked." Declan's grinning now, moving his shells across the board and ending on an empty one.

"I wasn't—" I stop, realizing he's messing with me. "Shut up and play."

He laughs. "Just making conversation."

I proceed to drop a shell into each subsequent hole until I land on an empty hole on my side, claiming all the shells on the opposite side. "How's Highland doing?"

"Good. Busy. We're adding two new programs in the spring—youth entrepreneurship and a financial literacy initiative." He's letting me change the subject, which I appreciate. "Maya's underwater with the planning, but she's in her element. You know how she gets when she has a project."

"Intense and unstoppable?"

"Exactly." He studies the board. "She wants you to come by sometime. See what we've done with the community garden space."

"I'd like that." And I mean it. Highland Community Center is Maya's life's work, and seeing what they've built there is always impressive. "Just let me get through this first month with the compliance assessment. Things are chaotic."

"Fair enough." Declan makes his next move. "Though Maya also said, and I quote, 'Elliot needs to remember he has a life outside Pierce.'"

"I do have a life."

"Do you? When's the last time you did something that wasn't work-related?"

"I'm here, aren't I?"

"Playing a strategy game with your best friend while talking about work is still basically work," he says, grinning. "I'm just saying—don't let this CEO thing consume everything."

"Noted." I proceed to drop a shell in each of the holes on the board. "Now can we focus on the game? Because I'm about to beat you again."

5

———

Cassie

Elliot's already in the conference room when I arrive, talking with Colton who looks to be in his forties. Tall, dark hair, tailored suit.

They both look up as I pull up a chair closest to the wall. As an observer, it's the best spot in a conference room with its floor-to-ceiling windows overlooking downtown LA.

"Good morning," Elliot says.

"Good morning," I say, setting my laptop on the desk. "Oh, and don't mind me. I'm here to take notes on processes."

Three weeks into my job at Pierce Enterprises, and this is my first operational leadership meeting observation.

It's standard compliance protocol—observing how decisions actually get made versus how procedures say they should be made. I've sat in dozens of these meetings at previous companies, watching executives navigate strategy discussions, resource allocation, interdepartmental conflicts.

But I've never observed someone I used to mentor.

Someone whose career I helped shape when he was still figuring out who he wanted to be.

Other executives filter in over the next few minutes. Colton sits to Elliot's right. A woman I recognize from an earlier meeting—Diane something, VP of Development—takes a seat across from them. Two others I haven't met yet. And then Harrison Gordon walks in, moving with the casual confidence of someone who's been in rooms like this for thirty years.

He sees me immediately. His gaze holds for just a beat too long before he nods and takes his seat at the opposite end of the table from Elliot.

"Let's get started," Elliot says, and the energy in the room shifts. Everyone focuses. "We've got a lot to cover. Colton, walk us through Q3 projections."

For the next forty-five minutes, I watch Elliot lead.

And he's good. Really good.

Colton presents financial data that's concerning—projections are down three percent from target, largely due to delays in the Blaisdell merger. Elliot asks precise questions, drilling into the assumptions behind the numbers without being aggressive about it. When Diane tries to deflect blame to the legal team for the delays, he redirects firmly but respectfully.

"The legal team is doing exactly what they should be doing—thorough due diligence. The timeline issues are on us for not building in adequate buffer. What's our mitigation strategy?"

Diane presents three options. Elliot evaluates each one, solicits input from the team, makes a decision. Clear, definitive, with reasoning articulated so everyone understands the logic.

This is what I saw potential for seven years ago. Strategic thinking combined with emotional intelligence. The ability to hold people accountable without making it personal. Leadership that invites collaboration while maintaining authority.

I'm taking notes, documenting the decision-making process, but part of me is just... impressed.

Then Harrison speaks.

"Before we move on," he says, his tone casual, "I want to circle back to something. Elliot, you mentioned requiring a community impact assessment for the Westside property?"

Elliot's expression doesn't change, but something in the room's energy shifts. "That's right."

"Help me understand why. We've never done that for smaller acquisitions. This property is what—thirty-eight million? We usually only require those assessments on deals over fifty."

It's a challenge dressed as a question. Everyone in the room knows it.

"Because we can't afford another Anderson Project," Elliot says evenly. "We're adding more checks on development deals. That was part of the changes the board approved last quarter."

"Right, because of what happened with Declan." Harrison leans back. "I'm just wondering if we're going overboard. Slowing things down when we don't need to."

"I'd rather slow things down than have another disaster."

"Sure, I get that. But this specific requirement—the community assessment for smaller properties—that wasn't in the original proposal, was it? You added that after the board meeting." Harrison's tone is still casual, but there's an edge underneath. "Which is fine, you're the CEO. I'm just asking—" He glances at me. "—since we have our Chief Compliance Officer here—whether you think this is good judgment or if you're overreacting because of what happened with your cousin."

The trap is elegant. He's questioning Elliot's judgment in front of me—the person whose entire job is to assess exactly that. If I don't respond, it looks like I'm giving Elliot a pass. If I do respond, I'm stepping into their power struggle on my first day.

Elliot meets Harrison's gaze directly. "I think it's learning from a mistake and making sure it doesn't happen again. If you've got actual data showing these assessments are killing deals, bring it to me and we'll look at it. But we're not dropping protections just because they're inconvenient."

The response is clean, direct. Non-defensive.

Harrison's jaw tightens slightly, but he nods. "Fair enough."

The meeting continues. More agenda items, more decisions. Through it all, I'm aware of Harrison's attention flickering toward me periodically. Watching how I react to Elliot. Cataloging my responses.

It's as if he's looking for evidence he can use against me or Elliot—or both of us—most likely due to whatever connection we had at Stanford.

By the time the meeting ends ninety minutes later, I have pages of notes about operational processes and decision-making protocols. And one very clear conclusion: Elliot is doing an excellent job as CEO.

Which means my eventual assessment is going to reflect that.

Which means Harrison is going to claim bias.

Perfect.

I SPEND the rest of the afternoon in my office reviewing documentation, building out my assessment framework, trying not to think about the political minefield I'm navigating.

By seven PM, the executive floor is mostly empty. I should go home. I've been here since eight this morning, and my eyes are starting to blur from staring at compliance protocols.

But as I stand at my window, looking at the LA skyline lit up against the darkening sky, there's something satisfying about this work. The intellectual challenge of understanding complex systems, identifying gaps, designing better frameworks. It's the kind of work I've always loved—the kind I'll miss when I walk away in six months.

Suddenly there's a knock on my doorframe and I turn away from the window to see Elliot, his tie loosened, his shirtsleeves rolled up.

"You're still here," he says.

"So are you."

"Yeah." He leans against the doorframe. "Colton and I were reviewing the Blaisdell numbers again. Trying to figure out how to make up that three percent gap without cutting essential operational costs."

"Any luck?"

"Some. Mostly we just gave ourselves headaches." He pauses. "You hungry? I was about to order dinner. Thai place down the street delivers."

I should say no. Should maintain boundaries, go home, keep this professional.

But I'm starving, and the idea of eating alone in my apartment is depressing, and it's just dinner. Colleagues eat dinner together all the time.

"Sure," I hear myself say. "Thai sounds good."

Twenty minutes later we're in the small conference room off his office—the informal one he showed me yesterday—with containers of pad thai and green curry spread between us.

"So," Elliot says, opening his curry. "Three weeks in. Have you had a chance to actually see LA? Or have you just been buried in compliance documentation?"

"Mostly buried in documentation," I admit. "I've been to the grocery store and back to my apartment. That's about it."

"You need to get out. See the city. It's got more to offer than just traffic and smog."

"Is that the official LA tourism pitch?"

He laughs. "I'm serious. There are great hiking trails if you're into that. Griffith Park, Runyon Canyon. The Hollywood sign hike is touristy but actually pretty nice, especially early morning before it gets crowded."

"I used to hike a lot in San Francisco," I say, surprising myself with the admission. "Been meaning to get back into it, but I haven't had time."

"Make time. It's good for clearing your head when work gets intense." He pauses. "Which, given that you're assessing whether Pierce's CEO is competent, I'm guessing work is pretty intense."

"You're fishing for compliments."

"I'm fishing for honest feedback from someone whose opinion I trust."

The sincerity in his voice catches me off guard. He genuinely wants to know what I think.

"You're doing well," I say carefully. "The meeting this morning showed strong strategic thinking, good people management, clear decision-making processes. If all your leadership meetings look like that, my assessment is going to reflect positively."

"But...?"

"But I need to be scrupulous about objectivity," I reply, "If my assessment is positive, Harrison might claim bias because of our history. So I need to make sure everything I document is airtight."

"That's going to make your job harder."

"It's going to make both our jobs harder." I take a bite of pad thai, thinking. "Professional distance, documented interactions, no situations that could be misinterpreted."

"Understood." He's quiet for a moment. "Look, I appreciate you taking this seriously. A lot of people in your position would just ignore the optics and do the job however they wanted."

"I'm not most people."

"I remember." There's warmth in his voice that makes something flutter in my chest. Dangerous territory.

I redirect. "So. Thirty-two years old, CEO of a major company. I would have thought you'd be married by now. Settled down."

It's meant to be casual conversation, but the moment I say it, I realize it sounds more personal than I intended.

Elliot raises an eyebrow. "Would you?"

"You always seemed like the type. Ambitious, but also... I

don't know. Like you wanted the whole package. Career, family, the works."

"I did. I do. Turns out the career part is easier than the relationship part." He sets down his fork. "I was with someone—Cecilia—for two years. Ended about six months ago."

"What happened?"

"She wanted commitment. Marriage, kids, the whole timeline, but I wasn't ready." He's quiet for a beat. "Actually, I don't know if I wasn't ready or if I just wasn't sure she was the right person. Either way, she gave me an ultimatum and I... couldn't commit. So we ended it."

"That must have been hard," I say.

It was. But then the interim CEO nomination happened and I had my work cut out for me. Maybe the relationship would have been doomed anyway." He says it like he's trying to convince himself. "What about you? I would have thought you'd be married with a couple of kids by now. I mean, you were engaged back at Stanford."

I nod. "For six years."

"That's a long time."

"Tell me about it," I say, chuckling dryly. "Brad kept saying we'd get married when the timing was right, when his business was more established, when I made partner, when... whatever. There was always a reason to wait."

"What happened?"

I take a breath. This is the part I don't usually talk about. "I turned forty. Started thinking seriously about kids. Brad said I was too old, that if we wanted kids we should have started years ago, that he didn't want to be an old dad." The words come out more bitter than I intend. "Then I caught him sleeping with his assistant."

"Jesus, Cassie. I'm sorry."

"Don't be. I'm better off without someone who saw me as having an expiration date—and no integrity." I'm surprised by how much I mean it. "The engagement ending was actually clarifying. Made me realize I'd been waiting for someone else to decide when my life could move forward. So I stopped waiting."

"And now?"

"And now I'm here for six months, then I'm pursuing the personal plans I've been putting off." I don't elaborate. He doesn't need to know about the fertility appointments, the donor selection, the whole plan I've mapped out for single motherhood.

Elliot's watching me with an expression I can't quite read. "You're not going to consider staying?"

"Six months," I reply, "That's the plan."

"That's... definitive."

"I've learned that waiting for the perfect moment means never actually doing anything. So I'm not waiting anymore." I meet his eyes. "I have a life I want to build, Elliot. And it doesn't include corporate compliance work indefinitely."

He nods slowly, like he's processing something. "That makes sense. I just... I guess I assumed you'd want to see the work through. The compliance frameworks, the system improvements. Six months feels like just enough time to identify problems, not enough time to really fix them."

"Then you'll have to hire someone permanent to finish the work."

"Or convince you to stay," he says, grinning.

"You won't," I say firmly. "But you'll find someone good to take over. Someone without complicated history who can do the job without Harrison breathing down their neck."

The mention of Harrison shifts the energy again. Back to reality, back to the complications we're navigating.

Elliot leans back, running a hand through his hair. "I'm glad you're here, Cassie. Even with the mess."

The sincerity in his voice does something to my chest. Something I should definitely not be feeling.

"I should go," I say, standing up and gathering the empty containers. "It's late, and we both need sleep."

"Right. Yeah." He stands too, helping clear the table even though I was clearly trying to make a quick exit. "Cassie—"

"Yeah?"

He pauses, seeming to weigh whether to say whatever he's thinking. Then: "Thanks for being honest about the situation we're in."

"Of course," I say. "And thanks for dinner."

I leave before the moment can stretch into anything more complicated.

Back in my apartment an hour later, I pour a glass of wine and call Lauren.

She picks up on the second ring. "Please tell me you're calling with gossip. I need entertainment."

"Not gossip. Just checking in."

"Liar. You never 'just check in.' What's wrong?"

"Nothing's wrong. The job is good. Challenging."

"And?"

Lauren knows me too well.

"And it's complicated," I admit. "The CEO is someone I mentored in business school seven years ago. I disclosed the connection to the board, but one of the other executives dismissed it as irrelevant. Now I'm wondering if he did that deliberately so he can use it against me later."

"That's... devious."

"That's corporate politics."

"And the CEO? The one you mentored? Is he making things weird?"

I think about tonight. The dinner, the conversation, the moment when Elliot said he was glad I was here and something in my chest responded.

"No," I say. "He's being professional. We're both being professional."

"But?"

"But nothing. It's just complicated to work with someone you have history with. Even professional history."

Lauren's quiet for a moment. "Are you attracted to him?"

"No." The answer comes too quickly. "No, I'm just aware that the situation requires careful boundary management. That's all, and I have plans."

"If you say so."

"I do say so. And speaking of plans—I have my fertility consultation in San Francisco next week. Tuesday afternoon."

"Oh! That's exciting. You're really doing this."

"I'm really doing this." Saying it out loud makes it real. Makes the timeline concrete. "Six months here, then I start the IUI process. By this time next year, I could be pregnant."

"I'm so happy for you, Cass," she says. "You're going to be an amazing mom."

"I hope so."

We talk for a few more minutes about logistics—travel plans, what questions to ask at the consultation, whether I should start looking at cribs yet (Lauren says yes, I say that's premature).

By the time we hang up, I feel grounded again. Reminded of what I'm actually doing here.

Six months. Prove I can still do this work at the highest level. Then walk away to build the life I actually want.

No distractions. No complicated feelings about former students who grew up to be impressive CEOs.

Just the plan. Stick to the plan.

6

———

Elliot

THE PARKING LOT at Griffith Park is already half full when I arrive at eight AM on Saturday. Not surprising—it's early October, perfect hiking weather, and everyone in LA has the same idea about escaping into the hills for a few hours.

I've been coming here since I was a kid. My mom used to bring us—me and my sisters—on weekend mornings before the heat got unbearable. We'd hike up to the Observatory, and she'd point out the native plants along the trail--California sagebrush, black sage, laurel sumac.

I haven't thought about those trips in years. Not until Highland started surfacing memories I'd buried under business school ambition and corporate success.

Today I just need to clear my head. Two months as permanent CEO, countless decisions, endless board politics, and Harrison's constant undermining. Plus Colton riding me about the Q4 projections, and the Blaisdell merger that's taking twice as long as it should.

And Cassie.

No, I'm not thinking about Cassie.

Except I've been thinking about Cassie for three weeks, ever since that Thai dinner in the office where she told me about Brad and her plans to leave after six months. I've been noticing when she stays late—which is often. Glancing toward her office when I walk past, even though there's no legitimate reason to check if she's there. Finding excuses to stop by her office that are professional but probably transparent.

She took two days off this week. Wednesday and Thursday. I noticed because Colton mentioned needing compliance sign-off on something and her office was dark. She'd told her assistant she'd be in San Francisco but didn't elaborate.

I don't know why she went to San Francisco. It's none of my business. She has personal plans she's pursuing—she said so explicitly. Those plans don't include me.

So I'm hiking. Clearing my head. Focusing on the fact that I have a company to run and a board member actively trying to undermine me. That's enough to think about without adding complicated feelings for my Chief Compliance Officer.

I lock my car and head toward the trail.

I'M ABOUT forty minutes in, past the worst of the tourist crowds, when I see her.

Cassie's about fifty yards ahead on the main trail, moving slowly in a cluster of people all trying to take photos of the Hollywood sign. She's wearing hiking pants and a tank top, her hair pulled back in a ponytail, looking frustrated as she tries to navigate around a family blocking the entire path.

I could turn around. Take a different trail. Pretend I didn't see her.

Instead I find myself walking faster, closing the distance. "Cassie?"

She turns, surprised. When she sees me, something flickers across her face—surprise, then pleasure, then something more guarded. "Elliot. Hi."

"Didn't expect to run into you here."

"Yeah, I thought I'd try hiking. Lauren—my best friend—keeps telling me I need to get out of my apartment on weekends. But while there's always the beach, I realized I haven't checked out the Hollywood sign at all." She gestures at the crowded trail ahead. "Unfortunately, everyone else has the same idea."

I glance at the path ahead, then at the smaller trail branching off to the left. "You want a better view? Less crowded, better angle on the sign. Like, from right behind it."

She hesitates. "I don't want to interrupt your hike."

"You're not. I was just wandering anyway." It's mostly true. "Come on. I'll show you the good stuff."

The trail I lead her to is narrower, steeper, but infinitely better. Within ten minutes we've left the crowds behind, climbing through scrub brush and California sage toward a ridge that offers a clear view of both the Hollywood sign and the downtown skyline.

"Are you doing okay?" I ask as I pause at a switchback, letting her catch up. "We can slow down."

"I'm fine. Just out of practice." She's breathing hard but smiling.

We keep climbing. The conversation flows easily—work, LA versus San Francisco, the weirdness of California seasons where October feels like summer. It's comfortable in a way that surprises me. Like we're just two people hiking, not CEO and compliance officer navigating complicated professional boundaries.

At the top of the ridge, I stop. "Here."

The view opens up—the Hollywood sign right below us, close enough to read clearly, the entire LA basin spreading out beyond it, downtown's skyline sharp against a rare smog-free sky.

Cassie catches her breath, staring. "Wow."

"Best view in the park. And no crowds."

"This is incredible." She pulls out her phone, takes a few photos, then just stands there taking it in. "I can see why your mom brought you here."

"She loved it up here," I say. "She always reminded me that LA was more than just traffic and concrete. That there was still nature if you knew where to look."

Cassie glances at me. "You miss her."

"Every day," I say softly. "She died three years ago. Cancer. It was fast—six months from diagnosis to gone."

"I'm so sorry, Elliot."

We're quiet for a moment, looking out at the city.

"She would have liked you," I say, surprising myself. "She always told me to surround myself with people who challenged me to think bigger. You did that. At Stanford, you were the one professor who wouldn't let me coast on potential. You made me actually work for it."

"You made it easy. You were one of the smartest students I ever mentored." She turns to look at me. "And look at you now. CEO at thirty-two. She'd be proud."

The way she says it—simple, genuine—does something to my equilibrium. Makes me aware of how close we're standing, how the breeze is pulling strands of hair loose from her ponytail, how different she looks out here compared to the boardroom.

I should step back. Create distance. Remember why this is complicated. Instead I hear myself say, "Have you been to the Observatory yet?"

"No. I keep meaning to, but—"

"We should go. It's right there, and it's Saturday. When else are you going to have time?"

She hesitates, and I can see her weighing it. Professional boundaries versus a beautiful day and a place she wants to see.

"Okay," she says finally, adjusting her hat. "Yeah. Let's go."

GRIFFITH OBSERVATORY on a Saturday morning is busy but not overwhelming. We wander through the exhibits—the Tesla coil demonstration, the Foucault pendulum, the planetarium show times posted on the wall.

Cassie's fascinated by everything. Asking questions, reading every placard, genuinely engaged in a way that's endearing. Like she's someone who actually loves learning, not just someone going through the motions of a tourist attraction.

"Did you know," she says, reading from a display about the Hubble telescope, "that the Hubble can see galaxies formed just a few hundred million years after the Big Bang? We're literally looking back in time."

"I did not know that."

"It's incredible. All of this—" She gestures at the exhibit. "—exists whether we understand it or not. We're just these tiny specks on a rock floating through space, and somehow we figured out how to look at other rocks floating through space billions of miles away."

"That's very philosophical for a Saturday morning."

"I'm a philosophical person." She's smiling now, that slight smile that transforms her whole face. "Brad used to say I asked too many existential questions. He preferred concrete answers."

"Brad sounds boring."

"He was. I just didn't realize it until it was over." She moves to the next exhibit. "What about you? Are you a concrete answers person or an existential questions person?"

"Depends on the context. In business, concrete answers. In life..." I pause, thinking. "I think I used to be more comfortable with ambiguity. When I was younger. Then business school and corporate life kind of trained it out of me. Everything became about metrics and outcomes and definitive strategies."

"You can train it back in," Cassie says. "If you want to."

"Is that your professional opinion as my former mentor?"

"That's my opinion as someone who spent too many years optimizing for the wrong things." She's looking at me now, something serious in her expression. "I spent my entire thirties building a career, waiting for the perfect moment to start my life. And then I turned forty and realized the perfect moment doesn't exist. You just have to decide what matters and do it."

"Is that why you're only here for six months?" I ask. "Because you decided what matters?"

"Yes."

"And what matters is...?"

She's quiet for a long moment. Like she's deciding whether to tell me or keep it private.

"Having a family," she says finally. "That's what I want. What I should have pursued years ago instead of waiting for Brad to be ready. So that's what I'm doing after my contract ends."

"That's... really clear," I say.

"It has to be," she says. "I'm forty-one years old, Elliot. I don't have time to be ambiguous about what I want anymore."

There's something both admirable and sad about the statement. Admirable because she knows what she wants and she's going after it. Sad because there's an undertone of urgency, like she's racing against time.

We keep walking through the exhibits. The conversation shifts to lighter topics—favorite planetarium shows we saw as kids, whether Pluto should still be considered a planet, the best science fiction movies about space.

It's easy. Comfortable in a way that makes me forget we're supposed to be maintaining professional boundaries.

We end up on one of the Observatory's terraces looking out at the view. Downtown LA right in front of us and to the west, the skyline of Century City with the ocean beyond it, hidden in the haze.

"This was a good idea," Cassie says, taking pictures of the view with her phone. "Thank you for suggesting it."

"Thanks for saying yes."

She glances at me, something in her expression shifting. Like she's suddenly aware of how long we've been together, how easily the day has unfolded.

"We should probably..." She trails off.

"Head back. Yeah." I don't move.

Neither does she.

There's a moment—just a beat—where we're both standing there, aware of each other in a way that has nothing to do with professional roles or compliance oversight or board politics.

Then someone bumps into Cassie from behind, breaking the moment. She steps forward, closer to me, and I automatically reach out to steady her. My hand on her arm, just for a second.

"Sorry," she says, stepping back quickly. "Crowds."

"Right. Crowds."

We head back inside, the easy conversation from earlier replaced by something more careful. Like we both felt that moment and we're both trying to pretend we didn't.

"We should probably head back," Cassie says. "It's a long hike down."

"Yeah. We should."

Taking a more direct route this time, the hike back takes an hour and a half. We take it slower than the climb up, and the conversation gradually finds its rhythm again—lighter topics, nothing too personal. But there's an undercurrent now, an awareness that wasn't there before.

By the time we reach the parking lot, it's mid-afternoon. The lot is packed now, families loading into cars, hikers streaming toward the trailhead.

Cassie's car is parked three rows over from mine. We stop between them, in that awkward space where goodbye should happen but neither of us seems ready for it.

"This was nice," Cassie says finally. "Unexpected, but nice."

"Yeah. It was." I pause, knowing I should just say goodbye and leave but not quite ready to. "Cassie—"

"Don't," she says quietly. "Whatever you're about to say, don't."

"You don't know what I was going to say."

"I do. Because I was about to say the same thing." She's looking at me with those eyes that are too perceptive, too knowing. "This was a good day. Let's leave it at that."

She's right. Whatever's happening—whatever we're both feeling—acknowledging it out loud would only make things more complicated.

"Okay," I say. "See you Monday."

"See you Monday."

I watch her drive away, then stand in the parking lot for longer than necessary, trying to figure out what the hell just happened.

7

Cassie

It's been four days since the hike with Elliot, and I haven't been able to stop replaying it.

The trail. The view. The easy conversation at the Observatory. That moment on the terrace when someone bumped into me and his hand steadied my arm, and for just a second we both felt it—whatever this thing is that's developing between us.

I've been avoiding him. Not obviously—I still attend meetings when required, respond to his emails professionally, complete my compliance assessments on schedule. But I've stopped working late. Stopped finding reasons to stop by his office. When I see him in the hallway, I keep moving.

When I don't have to be anywhere else that might have me running into him, I stay in my office and work.

Or review donor profiles on my laptop.

This is what I should be focused on. Not Elliot Walker. Not the way he looked at me on that terrace. Not the fact that I spent an entire Saturday with him and it felt like the most natural thing in the world.

Donor #4758: 6'1", brown hair, brown eyes, Master's degree in engineering, enjoys hiking and reading. Medical history clear. Three successful pregnancies reported.

Donor #4823: 5'11", black hair, hazel eyes, PhD in biology, plays guitar, avid runner. No genetic concerns flagged.

I should feel something looking at these profiles. Excitement. Anticipation. This is what I want—a baby, a family, the life I've been planning for months.

Instead I feel... detached. Like I'm reading a catalog instead of choosing the biological father of my future child.

My phone buzzes. Email from Melinda.

Subject: Executive Team Building - Friday

Cassie,

I'm adding you to this Friday's executive team building exercise. The board felt it would be valuable for you to understand team dynamics as part of your compliance assessment. Details below.

Location: Adventure Peak Ropes Course, Malibu Canyon Time: 8 AM - 4 PM Attire: Athletic wear, closed-toe shoes

See you Friday, Melinda

I stare at the email, my chest tightening with something that feels uncomfortably close to panic.

A full day. Eight hours. With Elliot and the entire executive team, doing trust exercises and team challenges and whatever other corporate bonding activities they have planned. In athletic wear instead of professional attire, which means I'll be seeing him in casual clothes again, which shouldn't matter but definitely does after last Saturday's hike proved exactly how distracting he is outside the controlled environment of boardrooms and business suits.

This is a nightmare.

I close the donor profiles and pull up my calendar, desperately hoping for a conflict. A scheduled site visit I'd forgotten about. A critical meeting I can't miss. A compliance deadline that would make attendance impossible. Anything that would give me a legitimate excuse to decline without raising suspicions about why I'm so desperate to avoid spending extended time with Elliot outside the office.

Friday is completely empty. Wide open. No conflicts, no excuses, no escape.

I could claim illness. A sudden migraine. Food poisoning that conveniently strikes Friday morning. Some medical emergency that would excuse my absence without requiring extensive explanation. It wouldn't even be entirely dishonest —the thought of spending eight hours navigating team building activities while hyperaware of Elliot's presence genuinely makes me feel nauseated.

But that would be cowardly. Obvious. Exactly the kind of behavior that would make Harrison Gordon wonder why I'm suddenly so eager to avoid team activities that include the CEO. He's already watching us too closely, looking for evidence that our past relationship is compromising my objectivity. Skipping a mandatory team building exercise would be like waving a red flag in front of him, giving him exactly the kind of ammunition he's been waiting for.

No. I'm going. I'm going to attend this team building exercise, participate professionally, maintain appropriate boundaries, and prove to myself—and to Harrison—that I can work alongside Elliot without it being complicated.

It's one day. Eight hours. I can handle eight hours.

I pull up the donor profiles again, forcing myself to focus.

Donor #4758. Engineering degree. Enjoys hiking.

Great. I close the laptop.
This is going to be a disaster.

ON FRIDAY, I arrive at the Adventure Peak parking lot by 7:45 AM, wearing hiking pants and a moisture-wicking shirt, my hair in a practical braid. Other cars are already here—Colton's Tesla, what looks like Melinda's Range Rover.

And Elliot's Audi.

Of course he's already here.

I grab my water bottle and head toward the check-in area, where a facilitator in an Adventure Peak polo is setting up equipment. About a dozen executives are gathered, drinking coffee and looking varying degrees of enthusiastic about the day ahead.

Elliot's talking to Colton, both of them in athletic gear that makes them look less like corporate executives and more like... regular people. Elliot's wearing a gray T-shirt and trail pants, his hair slightly disheveled in a way that shouldn't be attractive but absolutely is.

I keep my distance, checking in with the facilitator and accepting a harness and helmet.

"Cassie!" Melinda waves me over to where she's standing with two other executives I recognize from meetings—Tom Bradley from operations and Joanna Lim from legal. "Glad they included you. This should be interesting."

"Should be," I agree, trying to sound enthusiastic.

Harrison Gordon arrives exactly at eight, dressed in

expensive athletic wear that looks like it's never seen actual athletic activity. He surveys the group, his gaze lingering on me for just a beat too long before he moves to talk to Diane.

The facilitator—Jake, according to his name tag—calls everyone together.

"Welcome to Adventure Peak! Today we're going to work on trust, communication, and collaborative problem-solving through a series of challenges. We'll start with some low ropes course activities in teams, then move to the high ropes course this afternoon."

He explains the safety protocols, demonstrates how the harnesses work, divides us into three teams of four for the morning activities.

I end up with Colton, Diane, and Tom. Elliot's in a different group with Jennifer, Harrison, and someone from marketing I don't know well.

Relief floods through me. Different groups. I can do this.

THE MORNING low ropes challenges are actually... fun.

Our team has to navigate a series of obstacles—balancing on suspended logs, traversing a rope bridge, solving a puzzle while standing on unstable platforms. Colton is surprisingly athletic for a CFO who spends most of his time behind a desk; he clearly has a personal trainer, too. Diane's competitive in a way that's both amusing and slightly terrifying. Tom provides steady encouragement.

Even though I'm only here for six months, I can do this. I can be part of the team, participate in the activities, and maintain professional boundaries with Elliot, who's on the other side of the course with his group.

Except I keep catching glimpses of him. Laughing at

something Colton said when the groups cross paths. Helping Jennifer across a particularly tricky obstacle. Being the kind of leader who makes people feel capable and supported.

Stop looking at him, I tell myself. *Focus on your own team.*

By lunch, we've completed all the low ropes challenges. Jake gathers everyone for sandwiches and announces the afternoon plan.

"High ropes course! We'll be doing individual climbing elements with belay partners. I'm going to pair you up based on weight ratios for safety—"

He starts calling out names, and my stomach sinks.

"Cassie Reynolds and Elliot Walker."

Of course.

Elliot's across the group, and our eyes meet for just a second.

"Any problems with those pairs?" Jake asks cheerfully.

Harrison's watching us. I can feel his attention like a physical weight.

"No problems," I say, keeping my voice level.

"Great! Let's gear up."

THE HIGH ROPES course is about thirty feet up in the trees—a series of obstacles that climbers navigate while attached to a safety line controlled by their belay partner on the ground.

Jake and an assistant demonstrate the belay technique, showing how the person on the ground manages the rope, keeping it taut enough to catch a fall but loose enough to allow movement.

"The climber's safety is completely in your hands," Jake says. "This is about trust. The climber has to trust that their partner won't let them fall. The belayer has to stay focused and attentive the entire time."

Trust. Perfect.

Elliot and I move to our assigned climbing station. Jake checks our harnesses, confirms we both understand the belay system.

"Who wants to climb first?" Jake asks.

"I will," I say immediately. Better to get this over with.

I clip into the safety line, and Elliot takes position as my belayer, the rope running through the device on his harness that will catch me if I slip.

"On belay?" I call out, using the standard climbing communication.

"Belay on," Elliot responds. His voice is steady, professional.

"Climbing."

"Climb on."

I start up the first obstacle—a ladder made of logs suspended between trees. It's stable, easy enough. But as I get higher, the obstacles get more challenging. Swinging bridges. Platforms that tilt. Ropes to traverse hand-over-hand.

The whole time, I'm aware of Elliot below me, managing the rope, keeping me safe.

"You're doing great," he calls up when I hesitate at a particularly wide gap between platforms. "You've got this."

His confidence in me is... steadying. I make the jump, land solid, keep moving.

By the time I reach the final platform—a zip line that will take me back to the ground—I'm breathless and exhilarated and very aware that I just spent twenty minutes trusting Elliot Walker with my literal safety.

The zip line is fast, thrilling. I land on the platform at the bottom, and Elliot's there, helping me unclip from the line.

"Nice job," he says. His hand lingers on my arm for just a second longer than necessary as he steadies me.

"Thanks." I step back, putting space between us. "Your turn."

We switch positions. I take the belay device, Jake and his assistant double-check my setup, and Elliot starts climbing.

He's stronger than I am, faster. He moves through the obstacles with confidence, barely hesitating. But I'm intensely focused on managing the rope, keeping the right amount of tension, being ready to catch him if he slips.

He doesn't slip.

When he reaches the top and prepares for the zip line, he looks down at me. Even from thirty feet up, I can see his expression—something warm and trusting and entirely too intimate for a corporate team building exercise.

Then he's zipping down, landing on the platform beside me.

"Good belay," he says quietly.

"Good climb."

We're standing too close. I should step back. Create distance.

Jake appears before I can. "Great work, you two! How'd that feel?"

"Good," I say, stepping away from Elliot. "Really good."

"Trust is everything in belaying," Jake says enthusiastically. "You literally put your life in someone else's hands. That's the kind of trust we're trying to build in your teams."

He moves on to check another pair, leaving Elliot and me standing by the landing platform.

"Cassie—" Elliot starts.

"We should help pack up the equipment," I interrupt, not wanting to hear whatever he was about to say.

By four PM, the team building day is over. Everyone's tired, slightly sunburned, and—according to Jake's closing remarks—now a more cohesive executive team.

I manage to avoid any prolonged conversation with Elliot during the drive back. In my car, alone, I realize I just spent the day with Elliot. We were paired together. I trusted him to keep me safe while I climbed, and he trusted me to do the same for him.

And the whole time, I was hyperaware of him. The way he moved. The sound of his voice calling up encouragement. His hand on my arm when I landed.

This is bad.

I'm not just attracted to Elliot Walker. I'm developing feelings for him. Real feelings. The kind that make trust falls and belay partnerships feel like metaphors for something much more significant.

And I have absolutely no idea what to do about it.

THAT EVENING, Lauren calls.

"How was the team building thing?" she asks.

"Exhausting."

"Good exhausting or bad exhausting?"

I'm quiet for too long.

"Cassie. What happened?"

"Nothing happened. We did a ropes course, trust exercises, team challenges. Very standard corporate bonding."

"And?"

"And I was partnered with Elliot for the high ropes course. I had to belay him while he climbed."

"Belay?"

"Hold his safety rope. Keep him from falling."

"That sounds... intimate."

"It was professional," I say firmly. "It was a team building exercise."

"Yet you sound stressed, which means it wasn't just professional," she says. "What's going on, Cass?"

I close my eyes. "I think I'm in trouble."

"What kind of trouble?"

"The kind where I'm developing feelings for someone I absolutely cannot have feelings for," I reply, "My CEO. The person I'm supposed to be providing independent compliance oversight for. The person who's being watched by a board member looking for any excuse to question his judgment."

"Shit."

I sigh. "Yeah."

"How bad are the feelings?"

I think about today. The way my heart jumped when Jake announced we'd be partners. The focus I felt while belaying him, keeping him safe. That moment on the landing platform when we stood too close and I wanted to stay there instead of stepping away.

"Bad," I admit. "They're bad."

"Does he feel the same way?"

"I don't know," I reply, "Maybe? We spent last Saturday hiking together—completely by accident, we just ran into each other—and it felt like... something. But neither of us acknowledged it."

"Because you're both being professional."

"Because we're both being smart," I say. "I mean, I have a plan. Six months here, then I start the IUI process. I'm supposed to be choosing a donor, not developing feelings for my CEO."

"Maybe the plan needs to adjust."

"No. The plan is good. The plan makes sense," I say. "I'm forty-one years old, I want a baby, and I'm not waiting around hoping some man will decide I'm worth committing to. I learned that lesson with Brad."

"This isn't Brad."

"I know it's not Brad. But that doesn't matter," I say. "Even if Elliot had feelings for me—which I'm not sure he does—the timing is terrible, the optics are terrible, and a board member is watching us like a hawk waiting for us to make a mistake."

"So what are you going to do?" Lauren asks.

"I'm going to refocus. Do my job. Finish my six months. Start the fertility process like I planned." I say it firmly, like saying it out loud will make it true. "I'm not letting this derail what I actually want."

"And what you actually want is a baby."

"Yes."

"Not your CEO."

"It doesn't matter what I want," I say after a brief pause. "What matters is what's realistic. And a relationship with Elliot isn't realistic."

After we hang up, I sit on my couch with my laptop, pulling up the donor profiles again.

Donor #4758. Engineer. Hiking enthusiast.

Donor #4823. Biologist. Guitar player.

I should choose one. Lock in my decision. Move forward with the plan.

Instead, I keep thinking about Elliot's voice calling up encouragement while I climbed. The trust required to put my safety in his hands. The way he looked at me when he landed on that platform.

Stop, I tell myself. This is exactly what you can't do.

But knowing what I shouldn't do doesn't make the feelings disappear.

I close the laptop.

I'm in serious trouble.

8

Elliot

I'm FALLING for Cassie Reynolds.

Like, really falling.

Not just attracted to her, or professionally impressed by her. No, I'm actually falling for her in a way that feels completely different from anything I felt with any woman I've ever dated.

And I have absolutely no idea what to do about it.

I force myself to focus on Colton's latest quarterly projections for Q4. The numbers are good—better than good, actually. We're on track to exceed targets despite the Blaisdell merger delays, which means I can go into the board meeting next week with concrete evidence that the company is thriving under my leadership.

Harrison will find something to criticize anyway. He always does. But the numbers don't lie.

Outside my office, I can hear the usual sounds of the executive floor winding down for the evening—elevator chimes, footsteps in the hallway, the distant murmur of someone on a phone call. Most people have gone home already. Colton left an hour ago. Diane headed out at five sharp, something about a dinner reservation she couldn't miss.

But when I glance down the hallway, I can see light spilling from Cassie's office.

She's still here.

She's been working late a lot lately. I know because I've noticed—because I'm apparently incapable of not noticing everything about Cassie Reynolds. What time she arrives in the morning. Whether she stays late. The way she pulls her hair back when she's deep in concentration. The slight crease that appears between her eyebrows when she's reviewing something complicated.

I've been trying to maintain distance since the team building exercise. Trying to prove to myself that I can work alongside her professionally without these feelings getting in the way. We've had two meetings this week—both completely professional, both leaving me more aware of her than I was before.

I should go home. Leave her to finish whatever she's working on. Stop finding excuses to check if she's still here, to walk past her office, to manufacture reasons for conversation that are technically professional but mostly just me wanting to be near her.

Instead, I find myself heading toward the break room to make coffee. It's a legitimate reason to walk past her office. Completely innocent. I'm just getting coffee before diving back into the Q4 projections.

Except when I pass her door, I can see her through the glass wall, and she's not reviewing compliance documents or operational assessments. She's staring at her laptop with an expression I can't quite read—something between determined and uncertain, like she's trying to make a decision she's not entirely comfortable with.

I should keep walking.

I stop instead.

"Hey," I say, knocking lightly on her open door. "You're here late."

She looks up, and for just a second I see something in her expression—surprise, then pleasure, then that careful guard sliding back into place that she's been maintaining since the hike.

"Could say the same about you," she says, her tone light but not quite casual.

"Q4 projections. Colton wants me to review them before the board meeting next week." I lean against her doorframe, trying to look relaxed even though being this close to her makes my pulse pick up. "What are you working on?"

"Just..." She glances at her laptop, then back at me. "Compliance stuff. Nothing exciting."

It's not quite a lie, but it's not quite the truth either. I can tell from the way she said it—too quick, too dismissive.

"Want coffee?" I ask. "I was about to make a fresh pot."

She hesitates, and I can see her weighing whether to accept or decline. Whether maintaining distance is more important than caffeine and conversation.

"Sure," she says finally. "That would be great."

THE BREAK ROOM on the executive floor is small and well-appointed—espresso machine, premium coffee beans, a sitting area with comfortable chairs that no one actually uses during work hours. At seven PM, it's empty, just the two of us and the sound of the espresso machine heating up.

"How do you take it?" I ask, prepping the machine.

"Black. Two shots if you're making espresso."

"Hardcore."

"I've been working in corporate compliance for fifteen years. You don't survive that long without serious caffeine habits." There's humor in her voice, and something about being alone in the break room at night makes the atmosphere feel less formal than our usual interactions.

I make her espresso, then one for myself, and we end up sitting at the small table by the window that overlooks downtown LA. The city lights are starting to come on, the skyline glowing against the darkening sky.

"So," Cassie says, cradling her cup. "Q4 projections are good?"

"Better than good. We're exceeding targets across the board. Colton is cautiously optimistic, which from Colton is basically euphoric celebration."

She laughs, and the sound does something to my chest. "I've noticed that about him. Very measured emotional responses."

"It's his superpower. Nothing rattles him." I take a sip of espresso. "Your assessment is going well?"

"It is. I'm about halfway through the operational review. Should have preliminary findings ready in another month or so."

A month. Which means two months left on her contract after that. The timeline feels both impossibly long and terrifyingly short.

"And then?" I ask, even though I'm not sure I want to hear the answer.

"And then I finalize the report, present to the board, and

move on." She says it matter-of-factly, like it's already decided and unchangeable.

"To your personal plans."

"Yes." She doesn't elaborate, and I don't push.

"Thanksgiving is next week," I say, shifting to safer territory. "You have plans?"

"Flying to San Francisco. Spending the weekend with my best friend Lauren and her family." She smiles. "Should be good. I haven't seen them since I started here."

"That sounds nice. Long weekend?"

"Thursday through Sunday. Back Monday morning." She takes another sip of espresso. "What about you?"

"Hosting my sisters at my place in Eagle Rock. First time I've hosted a holiday since my mom died." I smile, thinking about the planning I've been doing. "My mom always made Thanksgiving a big deal—traditional American food plus Filipino dishes, both sides of our heritage represented. I'm trying to recreate that."

"That sounds wonderful."

"It's ambitious. I'm not sure I remember all her recipes." I pause, then hear myself say, "If you were in town, you'd be welcome to join us."

The invitation comes out before I've fully thought it through. But I mean it. I want her there, want her to meet my sisters, want her to be part of something that matters to me beyond board meetings and compliance assessments.

Cassie's expression softens. "That's really sweet, Elliot. But I'll be in San Francisco."

"Right. Of course." I try to keep the disappointment out of my voice. "Well, the invitation stands. If your plans change."

"Thank you."

We finish our espresso in comfortable silence, the conversation easier than it has any right to be given everything we're not saying.

"I should get back to work," Cassie says finally, standing up. "Thanks for the coffee."

"Anytime."

She heads toward the door, then pauses. "Elliot?"

"Yeah?"

"I'm glad you invited me. Even though I can't come. It means something that you asked."

Then she's gone, leaving me sitting in the break room with my empty espresso cup, trying to figure out what I'm supposed to do with these feelings.

It's almost eight PM when I finally finish the Q4 projections review and head toward the elevator. The executive floor is dark except for a few emergency lights and the glow from Cassie's office.

She's still here.

I should leave. Go home. Stop finding excuses to be near her.

Instead, I find myself walking toward her office.

The door is slightly ajar, and I can see her through the gap, but she's not looking at compliance documents. Her laptop is angled away from the door, but I can see the glow reflected on her glasses, liz she's scrolling through something with that same expression I saw earlier—determined but uncertain.

I knock lightly. "Still at it?"

She looks up, startled, and quickly closes whatever she

was looking at on her laptop. But not before I catch a glimpse of the screen.

Profile pages. Photos. Text blocks with information formatted like dating profiles but not quite.

I should make an excuse and leave. Pretend I didn't see what was on her screen. Maintain the professional distance we've been carefully cultivating.

Instead, I step into her office and close the door behind me.

"Donor profiles," I say quietly. It's not a question.

She closes her eyes briefly, then opens them to meet my gaze directly. "Yes."

"So that's what the personal plans are. After your contract ends."

"Yes." There's defiance in her voice now, like she's daring me to question her choice. "I'm going to have a baby. On my own. That's what I've been planning."

The words land with unexpected weight. A baby. She's not just leaving Pierce Enterprises—she's leaving to become a mother, and she's doing it alone.

"That's why you're only here for six months," I say, the pieces clicking into place. "You have a specific timeline."

"I do. I'm forty-one years old, Elliot. I don't have time to wait around hoping the perfect circumstances will material-ize. So I'm making it happen myself."

"How close are you to deciding?" I ask.

"Close. The appointment next week is to finalize every-thing and schedule the procedure." She's watching me care-fully, like she's trying to gauge my reaction. "This is happening, Elliot. I'm doing this."

"I know."

"And you think I'm crazy."

"I think you're incredible," I say, my delivery more enthusiastic than I'd wanted. "I think you know what you want and you're going after it, and that's more than most people ever manage. I think any kid would be lucky to have you as a mother."

Something in her expression shifts—surprise, maybe, then something warmer. "Thank you. That... means a lot." She pauses, her eyes narrowing. "But...?"

"But nothing. There's no but." Except there is, and we both know it. "I should let you get back to work."

"Elliot, wait." She stands up, moving around her desk. "I know that look and I know there was a 'but' there somewhere. So what were you going to say?"

We're standing in the middle of her office now, too close, the air between us charged with everything we've been carefully not saying for weeks.

"I was going to say that you're making a choice to do this alone, and I respect that. I do. But I wish..." I stop, trying to figure out how to articulate this without crossing every professional boundary we've been maintaining. "I wish the timing were different. I wish we'd met at a different point in our lives, when things weren't so complicated."

"Elliot—"

"I know. I know all the reasons this is impossible. You're leaving. I'm the CEO. Harrison's watching for any excuse to question my judgment. Getting involved would jeopardize everything we've both worked for." I'm saying all the rational things, but my feet are moving closer to her anyway. "But that doesn't change the fact that every time I'm near you, I have to remind myself why I can't do this."

Her voice is barely a whisper. "Do what?"

"This." I reach out, my hand hovering near her face but

not quite touching. "Tell you that I haven't stopped thinking about you since that hike. That belaying you last Friday felt like the most important thing I've ever done. That watching you make plans to leave in four months is the worst thing I can imagine."

Cassie's eyes are wide, her breath coming faster. "We can't."

"I know."

"This would be a disaster."

"I know."

"Harrison would—"

"I know." I'm close enough now that I can see the flecks of gold in her brown eyes, close enough to feel the warmth of her. "But right now, standing here with you, I don't care about any of that."

"You should." But she's not moving away. If anything, she's leaning slightly closer. "We both should."

"Tell me you don't feel this, Cassie." It's not quite a challenge, more like a plea. "Tell me I'm imagining it and I'll leave right now. I'll maintain professional distance, I'll stop finding excuses to be near you, I'll let you finish your contract and leave without making this complicated."

"I... I can't tell you that." Her voice is shaking.

I frown. "Why not?"

"Because I do feel it," she whispers. "I have been feeling it, and it's terrifying, and I don't know what to do about it."

I groan. "Fuck, Cassie—"

The sound of footsteps in the hallway makes us both step apart quickly, and I move toward the door like I was just leaving after a casual conversation.

The footsteps pass. Whoever it was didn't stop, probably didn't even notice the light in her office.

But the moment is broken.

Cassie leans against her desk, one hand pressed to her chest like she's trying to steady her breathing. I stand by the door, my hand on the handle, aware of how close I just came to cross a line I can't uncross.

"I should go," I say quietly.

"You should."

But neither of us moves.

"Elliot." She's looking at me with those eyes that see too much. "We can't do this. You know we can't."

"I know."

"So we're going to maintain professional boundaries," she says. "We're going to finish the next three months working together appropriately. And then I'm going to leave and pursue the life I've planned."

"Is that what you really want?"

She's quiet for so long I don't think she's going to answer. Then: "It's what makes sense."

It's not the same thing as what she wants. We both hear the distinction.

"Okay," I say finally. "Professional boundaries then. I can do that."

I'm lying and I'm sure she knows it. But she nods anyway, accepting the fiction we're both telling ourselves.

I leave her office and head for the elevator, but instead of going down to the parking garage, I find myself standing in the empty hallway, trying to process what just happened.

We almost kissed. We were seconds away from it, both of us leaning in, both of us wanting it despite every rational reason we shouldn't.

And if those footsteps hadn't interrupted us, I would

have kissed her. Would have crossed that line and damn the consequences.

The elevator chimes and I step inside, watching the numbers descend toward the parking garage.

Still, Cassie's right. We can't do this. The timing is terrible, the professional complications are significant, and she's leaving to pursue a very specific life plan that doesn't include a relationship with her CEO.

But standing in her office tonight, seeing the way she looked at me, feeling the electricity between us—I know with absolute certainty that professional boundaries aren't going to be enough.

9

—

Cassie

Almost.

A word that's been haunting me since that night two weeks ago when footsteps in the hallway interrupted something that would have been a complete disaster, seconds away from crossing a line we can't uncross.

The only problem is that while a part of me is grateful we were stopped—the rational part—the other part I'm trying very hard to ignore wishes those footsteps had never come. Wishes I knew what it would have felt like to kiss Elliot Walker instead of spending two weeks replaying the moment when we were so close I could feel the heat of him, see the want in his eyes that probably matched my own.

Alright, Cassie. Focus. You're supposed to be printing copies of your compliance report instead of daydreaming about kissing a man much younger than you. And who also happens to be someone you used to mentor.

The copy machine beeps, pulling me back to the present. I've been standing here for five minutes and haven't even started the print job yet. This is ridiculous. I'm a forty-year-old professional woman who's made a rational decision about her future.

I went to San Francisco over Thanksgiving, had my follow-up consultation at the fertility clinic, finalized my donor selection—Donor #4758, the engineer who enjoys hiking, though I'm trying not to think about why that particular detail influenced my choice. Everything is on track. The procedure is scheduled for April, right after my contract ends.

I have a plan. I'm sticking to the plan.

I feed the compliance report into the document feeder and hit print. The machine whirs to life, and I lean against the counter, trying not to think about the fact that Elliot's office light is still on, that he's probably working late too, that we're both here in this empty building avoiding each other while being completely unable to stop being aware of each other.

This is fine. Everything is fine.

The copy room door opens behind me.

I turn, already knowing who it's going to be before I see him.

Elliot stands in the doorway, a folder in his hand, looking as surprised to see me as I am—well, as I'm pretending to be—to see him.

"Cassie. Hi." His voice is careful, neutral, but something flickers in his expression when our eyes meet. "Sorry, I didn't realize anyone was using the copier."

"Just printing a report. Should be done in a few minutes." I gesture at the machine, which is steadily churning out pages. "You can wait or come back, whatever works."

He should leave. That would be the smart choice. We've

been successfully avoiding extended one-on-one interactions for three days now, and the copy room at seven PM when the executive floor is empty is definitely not the place to break that streak.

He steps inside and closes the door behind him.

"I can wait," he says, leaning against the counter opposite me. "No rush."

The machine continues its steady rhythm—whir, click, whir, click—filling the silence between us with mechanical noise that somehow makes the quiet feel heavier.

"How was Thanksgiving?" I ask, because I need to say something and small talk feels safer than the alternative.

"Good. Chaotic. My sisters are..." He smiles, and it's genuine, warm. "They're a lot. But it was good to have them at the house."

"I'm glad it went well."

"How was San Francisco?"

"Good," I say carefully. "Lauren's family is great. It was nice to spend time with them."

"And your appointment?"

I should deflect. Change the subject. Maintain the professional boundaries we've been carefully reconstructing since that night in his office.

Instead I hear myself say, "I finalized everything. Made my choice. The procedure is scheduled for April."

His expression shifts—something I can't quite read. "April. So right after your contract ends."

"That's the plan."

"You're really doing this," he murmurs.

I meet his gaze. "I told you, Elliot. I know what I want. I'm not waiting anymore."

He's quiet for a long moment, and I can see him processing, trying to figure out what to say that won't cross lines we've both been trying not to cross.

"I think you're going to be an amazing mother," he says finally. "Whoever that kid is, they're going to be incredibly lucky."

The sincerity in his voice does something to my chest. Makes it hard to breathe. Makes me wish—

No. I'm not going there.

"Thank you," I manage. "That means a lot."

The copy machine beeps, signaling it's finished. I should gather my documents and leave. Get out of this small room where the air feels too thin and Elliot is standing too close and everything I've been trying not to feel is pressing against my carefully maintained control.

I turn to collect the pages, and Elliot moves at the same time to set his folder on the counter. We end up reaching for the same spot, our hands brushing, and the contact is electric.

We both freeze.

I should step back. Pull my hand away. Do any of the sensible things I've been doing for three days to maintain distance.

But I don't move.

Neither does he.

"Cassie." His voice is rough, low. "We need to talk about what happened two weeks ago."

"Nothing happened."

"I almost kissed you," he murmurs.

"Almost doesn't count." But my voice is shaking, betraying the lie.

"It counts when I haven't been able to stop thinking about it since." He's closer now, close enough that I can see the exact shade of brown in his eyes, close enough to feel the heat of him. "It counts when I see you in meetings and all I can think about is what it would have felt like if those footsteps hadn't interrupted us."

"Elliot—"

"Tell me you haven't thought about it." It's almost a challenge. "Tell me you haven't been replaying that moment, wondering what would have happened if we hadn't stopped."

I should lie. Should tell him exactly what he's asking for—that I haven't thought about it, that it was just a momentary lapse in judgment, that we're both better off maintaining professional distance.

But I'm so tired of pretending.

"I can't tell you that," I say quietly. "But just because I have thought about it doesn't mean we can do this. We can't."

"Why not?"

"Because I'm your compliance officer," I whisper. "Because Harrison is watching us. Because I'm leaving in three months to have a baby. Because everything about this is complicated and messy and a terrible idea."

"I know all of that." He's even closer now, and I realize I've been leaning toward him without consciously deciding to. "But right now, standing here with you, I don't care."

"You should care. We both should." But I'm not moving away. If anything, I'm closer, drawn to him like gravity, like something inevitable I've been fighting against since that hike in October.

"Cassie." His hand comes up to cup my face, his thumb brushing across my cheek in a gesture so gentle it makes my breath catch. "Tell me to stop and I will. Tell me you don't want this and I'll walk away right now. I'll maintain professional distance for the next three months. I'll let you leave to pursue your plan without making this complicated."

His thumb traces along my jaw, and I can't think, can't remember all the rational reasons this is a bad idea.

"But if you don't tell me to stop—" His voice drops lower, rougher. "If you want this even half as much as I do, then I'm going to kiss you. And damn the consequences."

I should tell him to stop. Should step back, gather my documents, leave this copy room and never look back. Should protect my plan, my timeline, my carefully constructed future that doesn't have space for complications like falling for someone I'm supposed to be providing independent oversight for.

But I'm looking at Elliot, seeing the want in his eyes that mirrors something I've been trying to deny for weeks, and I can't make myself say the words that would send him away.

"I can't tell you that," I whisper instead.

"Then I'm going to kiss you now," he says, giving me one more chance to pull away, to stop this before it starts.

I don't pull away.

His mouth finds mine, and it's nothing like I imagined—it's better. Slower. More deliberate. He kisses me like he's been thinking about this for as long as I have, like he wants to memorize every detail, like he has all the time in the world even though we both know we don't.

My hands come up to his chest, feeling the solid warmth of him through his shirt, and then I'm kissing him back, all the restraint I've been maintaining for weeks dissolving under the pressure of his mouth on mine.

This is a mistake. A huge, complicated, potentially career-ending mistake.

But right now, with Elliot's hands sliding into my hair, his body pressed against mine, his kiss deepening until I can't remember why this was a bad idea—I don't care.

He backs me up against the copy machine, his hands bracketing my hips as he kisses me with an intensity that makes my knees weak. I can feel the edge of the counter pressing into my back, can hear the sound of our breathing filling the small room, can taste the coffee he must have had earlier on his tongue.

This is real. This is happening. And it's so much better than almost.

His mouth moves from my lips to my jaw, trailing kisses down the side of my neck that make me gasp. My fingers tangle in his hair, holding him closer, wanting more even though some distant part of my brain is screaming that we're in a copy room at the office where anyone could walk in.

"Elliot," I manage, though whether it's encouragement or warning I'm not entirely sure.

He pulls back just enough to look at me, his eyes dark with desire, his breathing as ragged as mine. "We should stop."

"We should."

Neither of us moves.

"Someone could walk in," he says, but his thumb is tracing circles on my hip through my skirt, his body still pressed against mine.

"The floor is empty." But even as I say it, I know how dangerous this is. How reckless. We're in the office where anyone could see us, where security cameras might be recording, where Harrison Gordon could walk in at any moment and have exactly the ammunition he's been waiting for.

The thought crashes through the haze of desire like cold water.

"We have to stop," I say, more firmly this time as Elliot closes his eyes briefly, then nods and steps back, putting space between us that feels both necessary and unbearable.

"You're right. I know you're right."

I straighten my clothes with shaking hands, trying to smooth my hair back into something professional. My lips feel swollen, my face flushed. Anyone who sees me right now will know exactly what I've been doing.

"This can't happen again," I say, trying to sound firm even though my voice is trembling. "This was—we shouldn't have—"

"Don't." He cuts me off, his voice rough. "Don't say you regret it."

"I should regret it. We both should." I force myself to meet his eyes. "Elliot, if Harrison finds out—"

"He won't."

"You don't know that. We can't control—" I take a shaky breath. "This was a mistake."

"Was it?" He's watching me with an intensity that makes it impossible to lie. "Because it didn't feel like a mistake. It felt like something I've been wanting to do since October when we ran into each other on that hiking trail."

"What we want doesn't matter. The timing is impossible, the professional complications are—"

"I know all the reasons this is complicated. But I also know that kissing you was the first thing that's felt right in months." He takes a step closer, and I force myself not to back away. "Tell me you didn't feel it too."

"What I felt doesn't change the reality of our situation."

"Which is what? That you're leaving in three months?

That you have plans that don't include me? I know, Cassie. I've known that from the beginning. But it doesn't change how I feel about you."

The words land with unexpected weight. How he feels about me. Not just attraction. Not just physical chemistry. Something more.

"Elliot—"

"I'm not asking you to change your plans," he says quietly. "I'm not asking you to give up what you want or compromise your timeline. I'm just asking you to be honest about what's happening between us. Because pretending it doesn't exist hasn't been working for either of us."

He's right. I know he's right. But acknowledging it out loud, admitting that this is more than just physical attraction —that feels dangerous in a way that even the kiss didn't.

"I don't know what you want me to say."

"Say you'll think about it. That's all." He reaches out, tucking a strand of hair behind my ear in a gesture that's too gentle, too intimate. "Just think about whether maintaining professional distance for the next three months is really what you want, or if you're just afraid of what might happen if we stop fighting this."

Then he picks up his folder from the counter and walks to the door. Pauses with his hand on the handle.

"Your report is still in the printer," he says, nodding toward the machine. "You should probably grab it before you leave."

And then he's gone, leaving me standing in the copy room with my heart racing, my lips still tingling from his kiss, and absolutely no idea what I'm supposed to do now.

10

Elliot

THE EMAIL from Colton arrives at three PM on a Friday, and I know immediately it's going to complicate my life.

Walk,

Blaisdell merger team needs us in San Diego Monday-Tuesday for final due diligence meetings. Client wants everything wrapped before year-end, which means we're on a tight timeline. I know it's last minute, but this deal is too important to delay.

Can you and Cassie make it work? We need compliance sign-off on their operational structure before we can finalize terms.

Flight details below. Hotel reservations at the Bayfront.

- Colton

I stare at the email, my cursor hovering over the reply button.

San Diego. Overnight. With Cassie.

It's been a week since the copy room. A week since I kissed her and felt her kiss me back with an intensity that's been replaying in my head constantly. A week of careful professional distance at the office—polite emails, brief interactions in meetings, both of us pretending that nothing fundamental changed when we both know everything did.

A week of catching her looking at me across the conference room and seeing the same want in her eyes that I feel every time I'm near her. Of working late and wondering if she's still in her office. Of replaying that kiss and knowing with absolute certainty that it wasn't enough.

And now Colton wants us to spend two days together in San Diego.

This is either the worst possible timing or exactly what needs to happen.

I forward the email to Cassie with a simple message: *Can you make this work? I know it's last minute.*

Her response comes back within five minutes: *Yes. I'll clear my schedule.*

Professional. Appropriate. Giving nothing away about what might be going through her head about spending two days with me after what happened in that copy room.

I reply to Colton confirming we'll both be there, then sit back in my chair trying to figure out if I just made a huge mistake.

Two days in San Diego. Client meetings during the day, but evenings and nights when we'll both be in the same hotel, trying to maintain professional boundaries that are already barely holding.

MONDAY MORNING ARRIVES cold and overcast, the kind of December weather that makes San Diego sound appealing. I'm at LAX by six AM for our eight o'clock flight, carrying my overnight bag and a folder of due diligence documents I should probably be reviewing instead of thinking about Cassie.

She arrives at the gate ten minutes after I do, pulling a small roller bag, dressed in professional travel clothes—dark pants, blazer, her hair pulled back in a way that should look businesslike but just makes me want to pull it loose and run my fingers through it.

Stop, I tell myself. You have to be professional about this. Two days of client meetings. That's all.

"Morning," she says, taking the seat next to mine at the gate. "Ready for this?"

"As ready as I can be for last-minute due diligence." I try to keep my tone light, professional.

The flight to San Diego is short—barely an hour—but it feels longer with Cassie in the seat next to me, close enough that I can smell her perfume, close enough that when the plane hits turbulence our arms brush against each other on the shared armrest.

She pulls out her laptop and reviews documents, making notes with focused concentration. I try to do the same with the due diligence reports, but I keep getting distracted by her presence—the way she tucks her hair behind her ear when she's thinking, the slight furrow between her eyebrows when she finds something questionable.

When we land, we head straight to the meetings. It's a long day—six hours of back-to-back sessions with the Blaisdell team, walking through financials and operations and compliance frameworks. But by the end of it, we have what we need. The deal is solid, the integration timeline is workable, and the client team is on board with the proposed terms.

The client dinner that evening is celebratory. Their CEO is pleased, Colton would be thrilled if he were here, and everyone's riding the high of a successful negotiation. Cassie and I play our roles perfectly—professional, competent, the kind of team that makes complicated deals look easy.

But under the table, I'm hyperaware of every time her knee brushes against mine. Every time she laughs at something the client says and I see the way her eyes light up. Every time she glances at me and I catch something in her expression that has nothing to do with merger negotiations.

By the time we're in the Uber back to the hotel at nine PM, we're both exhausted and exhilarated in equal measure.

"That went well," Cassie says, leaning back in her seat. "Better than I expected, honestly."

"You were impressive in there. The way you walked them through the compliance upgrades—they went from resistant to enthusiastic in about twenty minutes."

"That's because I made it about what they gain, not what they have to fix." She turns to look at me, and in the dim light of the Uber I can see the satisfaction in her expression. "This is a good deal, Elliot. If Pierce follows through on integration, this could be really successful."

"We will. Thanks to your assessment." I want to reach across the seat and take her hand, but the Uber driver is right there, so I keep my hands to myself. "You made this work."

The Uber pulls up to the hotel, and we head inside, crossing the lobby to the elevators. The adrenaline from the successful dinner is still humming through my veins, making everything feel sharper, more alive.

We step into the elevator alone, and the moment the doors close, the energy between us shifts.

We're standing close—closer than we need to in an empty elevator. Close enough that I can see the pulse at her throat, the way her breathing has picked up slightly.

"That was a good day," Cassie says quietly.

"Yeah. It was."

The elevator chimes for the eighth floor.

We step out into the hallway, and I realize for the first time that Colton booked our rooms across the hall from each other.

Room 816. Room 817. Directly facing.

We both stop in the hallway between our doors.

"Well," Cassie says, her voice slightly unsteady. "Goodnight, I guess."

"Goodnight."

Neither of us moves toward our respective doors.

"Cassie—"

"Don't." She cuts me off. "Don't say whatever rational thing you're about to say about why this is complicated or why we need to maintain boundaries."

"I wasn't going to say that."

She frowns. "No?"

"No. I was going to ask if you want to come to my room." I take a step closer. "Because I'm tired of being rational about this. I'm tired of fighting what I feel every time I'm near you. And if you tell me you want the same thing, then I'm going to stop thinking about all the reasons this is complicated and just... be with you."

Her breath catches. "We have meetings tomorrow morning."

"I know."

"If anyone finds out—"

"They won't. It's just us here. No one from Pierce knows

where we are or what we're doing." I reach out, running my thumb along her jaw. "Tell me what you want."

She closes her eyes briefly, and when she opens them, I see the decision made.

"I want to stop fighting this too," she whispers.

I unlock my door, and she follows me inside.

THE MOMENT the door closes behind us, everything changes.

I turn to face her, and for a second we just stand there in the dim light from the bedside lamp, both of us aware that crossing this threshold changes everything between us.

Then Cassie closes the distance, rising on her toes to kiss me, and rational thought disappears.

This kiss is different from the one in the copy room. That was restrained, careful, both of us holding back even as we gave in. This is unrestrained—weeks of tension finally released, no interruptions, no reasons to stop.

Her hands slide up into my hair, and I back her toward the bed, my mouth never leaving hers. She tastes like the wine from dinner and something uniquely her, and I can't get enough.

"Elliot," she breathes against my lips, the way she says my name undoing me.

"Cass," I murmur, wanting her attention. "Tell me to stop, and I will."

She pulls away. "Why would I tell you to stop?"

"I don't know. I'm just saying that if you wanted to stop, you can. This isn't a one-time thing for me. I'm invested."

Her fingers work at the buttons of my shirt. "I'm invested, too."

I'm not sure how to interpret her statement, so I lean

forward and capture her lips with mine. The kiss is intense, and it takes us a minute to slow things down. Cassie moans softly as my hand slides down her side, and I want to explore every inch of her body, every dip and curve.

Backing her toward the bed until the back of her knees hit the mattress, we fall onto it together. She gasps against my mouth and I swallow the sound, kissing her deeper, trying to show her without words what I'm feeling.

Want. Need. Something bigger than both that I'm not ready to name yet.

Her hands work my shirt, fumbling with the buttons and I help her—pulling it over my head and tossing it aside because I need less between us, need to feel her skin against mine.

"God," she breathes when her hand touches my bare chest, and the heat of her touch makes me shiver. "You're beautiful."

The word hits me in the chest, the unexpected compliment making me feel like a teenager who doesn't quite know what to do with his hands.

She pulls me back down, and the heat of our bodies is overwhelming. Her hips move, a soft grind against mine, and I'm already hard and aching for her.

She pulls her sweater over her head, and her bra-clad breasts are on display. They're full and round, the fabric straining over them.

"Cass, you're stunning," I tell her, and I reach out and trace a finger over her breast, watching her reaction.

She bites her lip, her hips rocking again, and she reaches up and touches my chin, her eyes locking with mine. "I want you."

"You have me."

Her hand trails down my neck, over my collarbone and across my chest. Her fingers are delicate, but the way she's touching me is anything but.

I work at the button of her pants, my hands steadier than they should be given how much I want this and she lifts her hips to help me slide them off. Then it's just her in exquisite lace underwear and a bra, and I have to stop for a second just to look at her.

"Don't," she whispers, and I can hear embarrassment starting to creep into her voice. "Don't look at me like that."

"Like what?"

She bites her lip. "Like... I don't know. Like you're cataloging every flaw."

"What flaw?" I lean down, kiss her slowly, thoroughly until she's making those small desperate sounds again. "I don't see any flaws."

"You're good." She smiles, a hint of shyness in the expression, as her hands work on the zipper of my pants. "You're so good."

"I'm right, though." I nip her lip. "You're perfect."

"Maybe we should stop talking now," she whispers as I reach behind her to unclasp her bra and she helps me, shrugging out of it and tossing it aside.

"Maybe." I kiss her collarbone, her sternum, learning what makes her gasp and what makes her hands tighten in my hair. When I take her nipple in my mouth, she makes a sound that goes straight through me—half gasp, half moan —and her back arches off the bed.

"Elliot—" My name in her voice like that does something to me. Makes me want to hear it again, makes me want to learn every way she can say it.

"Tell me what you want, Cassie," I say against her skin. "Tell me what you need."

"You," she gasps. "Just you. All of you."

As my hand slides down her stomach and into her panties, her eyes widen, her breath catching. I brush against her clit, my fingers stroking, dipping inside, teasing her.

"You're so wet." She's panting now, and I want to be inside her so badly it's almost painful. "I want to taste you."

She moans. "Please."

I kiss her again, long and slow, and then I'm working my way down her body, kissing her throat, her collarbone, her breast, sucking on her nipple as she writhes beneath me.

By the time I reach her center, her panties pulled down and tossed aside, her legs spread, I can smell her arousal. I kiss her thighs, the insides of them, teasing her. Her hands fist in the sheets, her hips rocking, and I can see her body tense and release, as if searching for something she can't quite reach.

I lean down and lick her center, savoring the taste, want and need and everything I've been denying myself for so long. When I lick her sensitive clit, her hands fly to my head, fingers tugging my hair as her back arches off the bed.

"Fuck," she gasps. "Elliot... please."

I suck on her clit, the pressure increasing, the suction pulling her closer to the edge. Her hips buck against my mouth as she moans my name, the sound loud and raw and so hot.

I slide one finger, then two inside her, stroking her, curling my fingers against her sensitive spot and her whole body tenses, her hips rising off the bed.

Then she's coming, her orgasm rippling through her, her fingers fisting the sheets. She gasps, her hips jerking, her muscles squeezing my fingers, and the sight of her coming apart like this is almost enough to make me lose control.

She's gorgeous when she comes, her whole body shaking with the intensity, and I stroke her through it, watching her come undone and feeling like I could die happy right here.

"Fuck, Cass," I whisper, and she smiles, her expression dazed and sated.

"That was incredible," she says, reaching for me. "You're incredible."

I kiss her, and she moans against my mouth, tasting herself on my lips, my tongue. She works at my jeans, sliding them off, then my boxer briefs, and the relief when she frees my cock is almost overwhelming.

Her eyes widen when she takes me in, and she strokes me, her hands firm and steady, her fingers brushing the tip. I'm close already, and I'm not even inside her.

"Cass, you have to stop," I gasp, and she immediately withdraws.

"Sorry."

"Don't apologize. Just—condom. Give me a sec."

She nods, and I grab a condom from my wallet, tear it open, and roll it on. Then I'm back between her legs, the tip of me nudging her entrance, and I'm looking down at her.

"Ready?"

"Yes."

I ease in, her muscles tight and warm, and she's perfect, everything I've imagined and more. Her hips rock up, her hands grabbing my shoulders, and I start to move, slowly at first, letting her adjust.

"Faster," she whispers. "Please, Elliot."

I speed up, thrusting deeper, and the sound of our bodies slapping together, the friction, the heat, is overwhelming.

She's moaning, her eyes locked with mine, and I can't look away. Can't do anything but watch her face as I thrust, faster, harder, trying to get closer, to go deeper.

She's coming again, and I can feel her muscles clenching around me, squeezing, and it's almost too much. I'm close, so close, and I can't stop, can't slow down.

"Cass," I moan. "Fuck—"

She pulls me closer, kisses me, and I'm lost, the wave crashing over me, my orgasm shuddering through me. I keep moving, her hips rising and falling, and we ride it out together, until the aftershocks are subsiding, and we're both breathing hard, covered in sweat.

When I can think again, I'm collapsed on top of her, both of us breathing like we just ran a marathon, her hands still on my back holding me close.

"I'm crushing you," I manage to say.

"I like it." Her voice is drowsy, satisfied. "You feel good like this."

I stay for another moment, just feeling the connection, then carefully pull out and deal with the condom. When I climb back on the bed beside her, she immediately turns toward me, curling up against my side and resting her head on my shoulder.

She feels perfect like this, and the moment feels so fragile and precious that I don't want to breathe, don't want to move, don't want to break the spell.

This wasn't just sex. This was claiming and being claimed. This was her trusting me with vulnerability she hasn't shown anyone in two years.

This was real.

"Are you okay?" I ask, because I need to know I didn't push too hard.

"I'm—" She takes a shaky breath. "I can't believe we just did that."

"Regrets?"

"No. Not regrets. Just—processing. It's been two years. Two years of not wanting anyone, not trusting anyone enough. And then you show up and I'm—" She stops, doesn't finish the sentence.

"You're what?"

She shakes her head. "Nothing. Just letting things happen instead of thinking too much."

Her vulnerability is beautiful. It makes me want to wrap her in my arms and never let her go, protect her from everything that could hurt her.

We lie there in the quiet, and eventually her breathing evens out and I realize she's fallen asleep. I should probably move, get up, put some distance between us before morning comes and reality crashes back.

But I don't want to move. I want to stay exactly like this—Cassie in my arms, her warmth against me, the weight of her reminding me that this is real despite the complications that await us in the morning, when we get back to LA.

I push the thought away, focusing on how perfect this moment is.

A moment I never want to let go.

11

Cassie

THE WEEK after San Diego feels like living in two worlds simultaneously.

In one world, I'm Cassandra Reynolds, Chief Compliance Officer, conducting operational assessments and attending board meetings and maintaining the careful professional distance expected of someone in my position. I respond to emails with appropriate formality. I present my preliminary findings with analytical precision. I sit in executive meetings taking notes while Harrison watches me like a hawk looking for evidence of bias.

In the other world—the one that exists in stolen moments and careful glances across conference rooms—I'm someone completely different. Someone who knows what Elliot tastes like. Someone who's memorized the sound he makes when I touch him. Someone who's counting down the hours until we can be alone again.

We've been careful. So careful. No one at Pierce knows what happened in San Diego, and we're both determined to keep it that way. We don't arrive at work together. We don't leave together. Our emails remain scrupulously professional. In meetings, we maintain appropriate distance, our interactions calibrated to reveal nothing beyond colleague courtesy.

But when the office empties in the evenings, when the executive floor goes dark and quiet, we find each other.

We've been limiting it to stolen kisses, heated moments that stop before they go too far. It's torture—after San Diego, after knowing what it's like to have him completely, stopping feels almost impossible. But my apartment is in a corporate complex where half the residents work in tech or finance. Someone could recognize Elliot's car, see him leaving at odd hours, mention it to the wrong person. His house feels too significant, too intimate, like going there would mean acknowledging this is more than just physical.

So we steal what moments we can in the relative safety of an empty office, and tell ourselves it's enough.

Tuesday night, it's his office. The door locked, the blinds closed, my back pressed against his desk while he kisses me with an intensity that makes me forget every rational reason this is dangerous. His hands slide under my blouse and I have to physically stop him, gasping against his mouth.

"We can't. Not here."

"I know." His voice is rough with frustration. "But God, Cassie, this is killing me."

"Me too." And it is. Every time we stop, every time we pull apart before going too far, it gets harder to remember why we're being so careful.

Thursday evening, it's the copy room again. The same place we first kissed, which feels both reckless and inevitable. We're supposed to be reviewing compliance documents, but the moment the door closes, professional intentions evaporate. His hands are in my hair, my fingers working at his tie, both of us breathless and desperate and completely unable to stop even though we know anyone could walk by.

"We have to be more careful," I say against his mouth, even as I'm pulling him closer.

"I know." His hands slide down my sides. "This isn't sustainable."

"No, it's not."

But neither of us knows what the alternative is. We're caught between the risk of being discovered and the impossibility of staying away from each other.

Friday afternoon, Colton stops by my office to discuss the Blaisdell merger integration timeline. I'm reviewing documents when he knocks, and I look up to find him leaning against my doorframe with his usual easy confidence.

"Wanted to thank you for being available last minute for San Diego," he says. "I know Elliot appreciated having your compliance insight on the ground during those negotiations."

"Happy to help. The trip was productive."

"It was." He pauses, and something in his expression shifts—just slightly, but enough that I notice. "You two work well together."

The comment hangs in the air for just a beat too long. Not quite an accusation, not quite innocent observation. Something in between that makes my pulse spike.

"We communicate effectively," I say carefully, keeping my voice professional. "Makes the compliance work easier when leadership is responsive."

"Right. Communication." Colton's mouth quirks slightly —almost a smile but not quite. "Anyway, wanted to update you on the integration timeline. We're looking at a Q2 start date, which means we'll need your compliance framework finalized by end of March."

End of March. Right when my contract ends.

"I'll have it ready," I promise, trying not to think about the fact that March feels both impossibly far away and terrifyingly close.

After Colton leaves, I sit at my desk with my heart still racing slightly. Does he know? Was that comment about working well together just professional observation, or did he pick up on something in San Diego?

We were so careful. Professional in public, no lingering looks during meetings, nothing that would signal we were anything more than colleagues collaborating on a deal.

But Colton's smart. Observant. It's what makes him excellent at what he does. And that comment—"you two work well together"—felt weighted with something I couldn't quite identify.

I force myself to focus on work, but my mind keeps drifting to Elliot. To San Diego. To the way he looked at me in that hotel room when he said I was worth the risk.

We haven't talked about what happens when my contract ends. Haven't discussed how this relationship—if that's even what we're calling it—fits with my fertility plans, my timeline for motherhood, the future I've been constructing that doesn't include space for complications like falling for my CEO.

We're living in the present, stealing moments when we can, and carefully not thinking about the fact that we're building toward something that has an expiration date.

My phone buzzes with an incoming text.

ELLIOT:

Conrad Hotel. Room 512. 8 PM?

My breath catches. Not the office. Not stolen kisses in empty hallways. An actual hotel room where we can be together without the constant fear of discovery.

It's riskier in some ways—checking in, being seen in a hotel lobby. But also safer than my corporate apartment complex or his house that we're both carefully avoiding for reasons neither of us has articulated.

I should say no. Should tell him we need to cool this down, maintain more distance, remember that every moment we spend together increases the risk of discovery.

Instead I text back: *I'll be there.*

I ARRIVE AT 8:15, intentionally late so I don't have to wait in the hallway. The elevator ride to the fifth floor feels interminable, my heart pounding harder with each floor. By the time I reach room 512, my hands are shaking slightly as I knock.

Elliot opens the door immediately, like he was waiting on the other side. His tie is already gone, his shirt partially unbuttoned, and the look in his eyes makes my knees weak.

"Hi," I manage.

"Hi." He pulls me inside, the door barely closed before his mouth is on mine.

It's different from the stolen moments at the office. No fear of interruption, no need to stay quiet, no stopping before we go too far. We have time and privacy and the freedom to take what we've been denying ourselves all week.

I'm already working at the buttons of his shirt, desperate

to feel his skin against mine. He's equally urgent, his hands sliding under my blouse, unclasping my bra with practiced efficiency.

"I've been thinking about this all week," he says against my neck, his voice rough. "Every meeting, every time you walked past my office, every professional email you sent—all I could think about was getting you alone."

"Same." I tug his shirt free, running my hands over his chest, his shoulders, relearning the planes of his body. "I almost lost it on Thursday. In the copy room. When you had me pressed against the door—"

"I know." His hands are at my waist now, unfastening my pants. "I wanted to lock the door and say fuck it to being careful."

"We can't do that."

"I know." He lifts me slightly, walking us backward toward the bed. "But we can do this."

We fall onto the bed together, a tangle of limbs and desperate hands and mouths seeking skin. There's no patience this time, no slow exploration like in San Diego. This is raw need, a week of pent-up frustration and denial finally finding release.

My blouse is gone, then my pants. His shirt hits the floor. By the time we're both naked, we're both breathless and desperate and done with any pretense of taking our time.

"Condom," I gasp as his mouth finds my breast. "Please tell me you have—"

"Wallet. Back pocket."

I reach for his discarded pants, fumbling for his wallet while he continues his assault on my senses—his mouth on my neck, my collarbone, his hands everywhere at once. By the time I find the condom and tear it open, I'm shaking with need.

He takes it from me, rolling it on with quick efficiency, and then he's over me, between my legs, looking down at me with an intensity that steals my breath.

"Cassie—"

"Don't talk." I pull him down. "Just—please—"

He slides into me, filling me, and it's a relief, a release, an answer to a question we've both been asking all week. I'm panting, my hips rocking up to meet his, and he starts moving, slow, steady, deeper.

"Harder," I gasp. "Faster."

He obliges, his thrusts picking up speed, his breathing changing, and it's so good, the friction and heat and pressure building, building.

I'm not going to last, not after a week of waiting, wanting, holding back. Not with the way he's touching me, his hands sliding over my breasts, my stomach, his mouth on mine, kissing me hungrily, desperately.

"Elliot," I moan, and I'm so close, so close—

And then he shifts, reaching between us, his fingers finding my clit, and I'm there, flying over the edge, my whole body shaking with the force of it.

He's still moving, and the sensation is overwhelming, almost too much, but I don't want him to stop. Not until he's there too, his whole body shuddering as his orgasm hits him, his lips pressed against my neck.

For a long moment, we stay tangled together, his weight pressing me into the bed, his breath warm against my neck, both of us breathing hard, shaking slightly from the intensity.

"We can't go a whole week like that again," Elliot finally

says, his voice muffled against my shoulder. "That was torture."

"Agreed." I run my fingers through his hair. "But we also can't do this every night. The risk—"

"I know." He lifts his head to look at me. "Next week? Here? We can rotate hotels, be careful about timing."

It's still risky. Still dangerous. But the alternative—going back to just stolen kisses that leave us both frustrated and desperate—feels impossible now.

"But we have to be careful. LA is small, when you think about it," I say. "No patterns someone could notice. Different hotels. Different times."

"Deal." He kisses me, softer now. Tender instead of desperate. "We'll make this work."

We clean up, and then we're both climbing back into bed, his arm around my waist, his mouth against my neck. In the morning, we'll have to leave separately, go back to our respective homes, and prepare to be professional colleagues again on Monday morning.

But for now, in this hotel room, we can just be Elliot and Cassie. Two people who can't stay away from each other despite every rational reason they should.

THE PATTERN CONTINUES through the following week. Careful professional distance during the day, stolen intimacy when the office empties at night. We're playing with fire, and we both know it. But neither of us seems capable of stopping.

It's the Wednesday before Christmas when everything shifts.

I'm in my office reviewing operational procedures when my phone rings. My mother's name on the caller ID.

"Hi Mom," I answer, already mentally preparing for the usual pre-holiday check-in about travel plans and what I'm bringing to Portland.

"Cassie, honey, I have some bad news." Her voice sounds tired, older than usual. "I came down with shingles yesterday. The doctor says I'm contagious for at least another week, maybe longer."

My stomach drops. "Mom, are you okay? Do you need me to come up there?"

"No, absolutely not. That's why I'm calling—you can't come for Christmas. I don't want you to risk catching this, and honestly, I'm not feeling up to hosting anyway." She coughs, and I can hear the exhaustion. "The staff here at the complex are taking good care of me. Susan from next door is checking in every few hours. I'll be fine."

"Are you sure? I can wear a mask, I can—"

"Cassandra." Her voice is firm despite the fatigue. "I'm sure. Stay in LA. Spend the holiday with friends. I'll be perfectly fine here, and we'll do Christmas when I'm better. Maybe in January."

We talk for a few more minutes, and she assures me repeatedly that she's being well cared for, that the facility staff are attentive, that her friends in the complex are bringing her meals and keeping her company from a safe distance.

After we hang up, I immediately call the Cascade Falls Senior Living facility and speak with the nursing staff. They confirm that my mother is stable, being monitored regularly, and has everything she needs. They'll call me if anything changes.

I should feel relieved. She's okay. She's being cared for.

Instead, I feel untethered. My Christmas plans just evaporated, and I'm looking at spending the holiday alone in my Los Angeles apartment, which suddenly feels more depressing than I want to admit.

I text Lauren: *Mom has shingles. Christmas in Portland is cancelled. She's okay but contagious, so I can't visit.*

Her response comes back within minutes: *Oh no! I'm so sorry. Come to SF! Spend Christmas with us!*

I check flights on my laptop. Everything is either sold out or absurdly expensive—apparently I'm not the only person whose holiday plans just changed. Driving to San Francisco would take six hours, and the thought of spending Christmas Eve on I-5 makes me want to cry.

ME:

> Flights are impossible and I don't want to drive 6 hours on Christmas Eve. But thank you for offering.

LAUREN:

> You're not spending Christmas alone!!!

ME:

> I'll be fine. I'll order takeout and watch movies. Very festive.

I'm staring at my laptop, contemplating whether Chinese food or pizza is more appropriate for solo Christmas dinner, when there's a knock on my office door.

Elliot.

"Hey," he says, stepping inside and closing the door behind him. "You okay? You've been in here with your door closed for an hour."

"My mom has shingles. Christmas in Portland is cancelled."

His expression shifts immediately to concern. "Is she all right?"

"She's fine. Being well cared for at her facility. But she doesn't want me to visit and risk catching it." I lean back in my chair. "So I'm apparently spending Christmas alone in LA."

"What about San Francisco? Your friend Lauren?"

"Invited me, but flights are impossible this late. I'm not driving six hours on Christmas Eve." I try to smile, but it feels forced. "It's fine. I'll survive a quiet Christmas."

"Spend it with us," he says, grinning. "Christmas. My sisters are coming—Keeley and her family, and Nina. We're doing the whole thing at my place in Eagle Rock. Big Filipino-American Christmas like my mom used to do." He pauses. "Come with me."

My heart does something complicated in my chest. "Elliot, I can't crash your family Christmas—"

"You're not crashing. I'm inviting you." He moves closer to my desk. "Look, I know it's a big step. Meeting my sisters is significant, and we've been keeping this private. But they already know I'm seeing someone—I told them after San Diego because Keeley wouldn't stop asking why I sounded so happy. I didn't give them your name or details, but they know."

"They know you're seeing someone you work with?"

"They know I'm seeing someone I care about who makes me happy." His voice softens. "And I'd really like them to meet you. If you're comfortable with it."

Meeting his family. This is so far beyond stolen moments at the office or a business trip to San Diego. This is real relationship territory—the kind where you integrate into each other's lives, meet important people, acknowledge that this is more than just physical.

"What would you tell them? About who I am, how we know each other?"

"The truth. That you're doing compliance work for Pierce, that we knew each other from Stanford years ago, that we reconnected and started seeing each other." He's watching me carefully. "They won't say anything to anyone. Keeley's a pediatrician, Nina teaches high school—neither of them has any connection to Pierce or the business world. And they're family. They'll keep it private."

I should say no. Should maintain boundaries, keep this contained, not let it expand into family gatherings and holiday celebrations.

But the thought of spending Christmas alone feels unbearable. And the thought of spending it with Elliot— even with his sisters there, even with the complications that creates—feels like exactly what I want.

"Okay," I hear myself say. "Yes. I'd like that."

The relief on his face is immediate. "Yeah?"

"Yes." I'm nervous now, second-guessing. "What should I bring? Do I need to cook something? Should I—"

"Just bring yourself. Keeley's handling most of the food —she's very particular about recreating Mom's recipes. I'm doing the lumpia and pancit. Nina's bringing dessert." He's grinning now. "Fair warning: they're going to interrogate you. Keeley especially. She's very protective."

"Great. No pressure."

"You'll be fine. They're going to love you." He glances toward my door, checking that it's still closed, then leans down to kiss me quickly. "Thank you for saying yes. This means a lot."

After he leaves, I sit at my desk trying to process what just happened.

I'm spending Christmas with Elliot Walker's family. Meeting his sisters. This is so far past casual or temporary that I can't even pretend anymore.

This is a relationship.

Real and significant and definitely more than I planned for.

12

Cassie

CHRISTMAS EVE ARRIVES with perfect Southern California weather—seventy degrees and sunny, palm trees swaying in the breeze.

I've packed and repacked my bag three times, trying to figure out what one wears to meet your secret boyfriend's family for Christmas when you're supposed to be keeping the relationship private from everyone at work.

I settle on casual but put-together—dark jeans, a soft sweater, the new boots I bought last month. My overnight bag has pajamas, toiletries, a change of clothes for Christmas Day, and the small gifts I bought for Elliot's sisters after obsessively googling "what to bring when meeting your boyfriend's family for the first time."

The drive to Eagle Rock takes thirty minutes through light holiday traffic. Elliot's house is in a quiet neighborhood with mature trees and Spanish-style homes, the kind of area that feels residential and established rather than trendy.

His house is beautiful—a charming Spanish-style home that rises three stories, painted in warm terracotta with white trim, tile roof, arched windows. The front has a small courtyard garden with a fountain, and the whole place looks like it's been lovingly maintained. Christmas lights outline the arched doorway and windows, and I can see a wreath hanging on the dark wood front door.

I park on the street and grab my bag, my stomach fluttering with nerves. Meeting his family. This is huge. This makes everything between us feel more real than it has since San Diego.

The front door opens before I reach it, and Elliot's there, wearing jeans and a casual button-down, barefoot, looking relaxed and happy.

"Hey," he says, smiling. "You made it."

"Traffic was easy." I step into the courtyard, and he takes my bag, then pulls me into a quick hug.

"You okay?" he murmurs. "You look nervous."

"I am nervous. I'm meeting your family."

"They're going to love you. I promise." He leads me inside. "Fair warning: it's chaos in there. Keeley's kids are running around, Nina's already had two glasses of wine, and everyone's arguing about whether the lumpia is as good as Mom's."

The house is even more beautiful inside. The entryway opens into a living room with exposed beam ceilings, tile floors, a large fireplace, and warm, comfortable furniture that looks lived-in rather than decorated. Through the archway I can see a dining room with a long table already set for dinner, and beyond that what looks like a kitchen where I can hear voices and laughter.

But what really catches my attention is the Christmas tree in the corner—at least eight feet tall, decorated with an eclectic mix of ornaments that look collected over years, some clearly handmade, some traditional, all of them hung with obvious care. String lights are draped around doorways and windows, and I can smell something amazing cooking—garlic and ginger and something sweet.

"Kuya!" A woman's voice calls from the kitchen. "Is that your girlfriend?"

Elliot grimaces slightly. "That's Keeley. She's subtle."

A woman appears in the doorway—mid-thirties, pretty, with dark hair pulled back in a ponytail and an expression that's both welcoming and assessing. She's wearing an apron over her clothes and holding a wooden spoon.

"You must be Cassie," she says, coming forward with a warm smile. "I'm Keeley. Elliot's told us absolutely nothing about you, which is very annoying."

"I told you some things," Elliot protests.

"You said 'I'm seeing someone' and refused to elaborate." Keeley turns back to me. "So we're all dying to know everything. Come in, come in. Ignore the chaos."

She leads me toward the kitchen, where another woman is chopping vegetables at the counter—younger than Keeley, maybe late twenties, with the same dark hair and warm eyes.

"Nina," she introduces herself, wiping her hands on a towel before shaking mine. "The baby sister. And those screaming children you hear are my niece and nephew, who Keeley promised would be well-behaved and clearly lied."

"They're four and six," Keeley says defensively. "Well-behaved is relative. Especially since their dad has them for New Year's, so they're extra wild knowing they get Christmas with us."

"First holiday season post-divorce," Nina adds quietly to me. "We're still figuring out the new normal."

"It's fine," Keeley says firmly, though there's something in her expression that suggests it's not entirely fine. "The kids are happy. That's what matters."

Two kids come racing through the kitchen—a little girl with pigtails and a slightly older boy, both clearly in the middle of some elaborate game.

"Mama says we can open presents tomorrow!" the girl announces to no one in particular before racing back out.

"After breakfast, Téa!" Keeley calls after her. Then to me: "Sorry. Christmas makes them feral."

"It's fine." I'm actually smiling now. There's something warm and chaotic and welcoming about this scene that makes my nervousness start to ease. "Can I help with anything?"

"You're a guest," Keeley says firmly. "Elliot, show her around. Get her settled. We're eating in an hour."

ELLIOT LEADS me up a beautiful tile staircase to the second floor. "Your room is up here," he says, carrying my bag down a hallway with more arched doorways and exposed beams. "I put you in the guest room—it has its own bathroom, and it's quiet since it's on the opposite end from the kids."

The guest room is lovely—a queen bed with a wrought-iron headboard, Spanish tile on the floor with a thick rug, a window that looks out over what must be the garden in back. There's a small en-suite bathroom through a door on one side.

"It's beautiful," I say honestly.

"My mom decorated most of the house after I bought it five years ago. I've kept it pretty much the same since she died." He sets my bag on the chair by the window. "My room is on the third floor if you need anything."

The third floor. Away from my room.

I give him a knowing look. "Elliot—"

"I know." He almost looks embarrassed as he steps closer, his voice dropping low. "I know we can't... I mean, with my sisters here, and the kids, we have to be careful. But I'm really glad you're here, even if we have to behave."

"I don't mind behaving." I touch his face, and he leans into it. "Thank you for inviting me."

He kisses me then, soft and sweet, and I let myself lean into it for just a moment before we both pull back.

"We should go back downstairs before Keeley comes looking for us," he says. "She's very nosy."

I giggle. "I like her already."

DINNER IS loud and chaotic and wonderful. Keeley's kids—Téa and Tanner—are adorable terrors who ask me approximately eight hundred questions about everything from my job ("What's compliance?" "Is it like being a police officer?" "Do you have a gun?") to whether I like their Uncle Elliot ("He's okay," I say diplomatically, and Elliot kicks me under the table).

The food is incredible—lumpia that's crispy and perfectly seasoned, pancit with the right balance of vegetables and noodles, adobo that tastes even better than what Elliot made on Thanksgiving when this was supposed to be just the two of us, and rice that's fluffy and perfect. There's also ham, because Keeley insists on having "at least one traditional American thing," and various side dishes that blend Filipino and American holiday traditions.

Throughout dinner, I watch Elliot with his family, and something in my chest aches. He's so different here than he is at Pierce—more relaxed, quicker to laugh, the CEO persona completely set aside. He teases his sisters mercilessly, is patient with the kids even when they're being ridiculous, and every so often catches my eye across the table with a look that makes me warm all over.

This is what family looks like. Not perfect, not formal, but loud and messy and full of love. The kind of family I always wanted but never quite had with just me and my mother.

The kind of family I told myself I didn't need when I decided to pursue single motherhood.

After dinner, we clean up together—Keeley washing, me drying, Nina putting things away, Elliot corralling the kids into the living room for a movie before bed. It's comfortable, this domestic rhythm, like I've been part of this family routine for years instead of hours.

"He's different with you," Keeley says quietly, handing me a dripping plate.

"What do you mean?"

"Elliot. He's... lighter. Happier." She's watching me with that same assessing look from earlier, but warmer now. "I haven't seen him like this since before Mom died. Maybe ever."

I don't know what to say to that, so I just focus on drying the plate carefully.

"I don't know what your situation is," Keeley continues. "He said it's complicated, which usually means impossible. But whatever you're doing—however long you have—thank you for making him happy."

The words land with unexpected weight. Because she's right—this is temporary, complicated, probably impossible long-term. But right now, right here, we're both happy.

"He makes me happy too," I say quietly.

Keeley smiles. "Good. That's all that matters then."

After the kids are in bed and Nina has retreated to her room with a book, claiming she needs "recovery time from all that family togetherness," Elliot and I end up on the back patio.

The house has a beautiful covered patio overlooking a terraced garden, and beyond that, a view of Eagle Rock that's more nature than city—rolling hills covered in chaparral and live oak, the lights from scattered houses twinkling in the darkness. It's quiet out here, peaceful, the kind of space that invites conversation.

"Your sisters are wonderful," I say, settling into one of the comfortable chairs. "And your niece and nephew are adorable terrors."

"They liked you." He's leaning against the patio railing, looking out at the view. "Keeley especially. She doesn't warm up to people easily, but she was relaxed with you almost immediately."

"She asked me if my intentions toward you were honorable."

He groans. "Of course she did. What did you say?"

"That my intentions were complicated but genuine." I pause. "She seems satisfied with that answer."

"She would be. Keeley's all about authenticity. As long as you're honest, she's fine with whatever."

We're quiet for a moment, and I'm very aware that we're alone for the first time since I arrived, that his room is upstairs and mine is down the hall, that his family is here and we have to be careful but god, I want to touch him.

"Come here," he says quietly.

I stand and move to where he's leaning against the railing, and he pulls me into his arms, my back to his chest, both of us looking out at the view.

"Thank you for being here," he murmurs against my hair. "I know meeting my family is a big deal. I know it makes this more real than we've been pretending it is."

"It is real," I say, and the admission feels significant. "Elliot, whatever we've been telling ourselves about keeping this casual or temporary—tonight made it pretty clear that ship has sailed."

"I know." His arms tighten around me. "Does that scare you?"

"Terrifies me." I lean back into him. "Because I'm still leaving in three months. I still have plans—the fertility procedure, becoming a mother. And being here with your family tonight, seeing what you have with Keeley and Nina and the kids... it made me realize how lonely my plan is."

He's quiet for a long moment. "What do you mean?"

"I convinced myself that single motherhood was the smart choice. That I didn't need a partner or a traditional family. That I could do it all on my own and be fine." I turn in his arms to face him. "But watching you with your sisters tonight, seeing how they support each other, how the kids have all of you—it made me realize what I'd be giving up. What my child would be giving up."

"Cassie—"

"I'm not changing my mind," I say quickly. "I'm just... acknowledging that maybe my plan isn't as perfect as I convinced myself it was."

He cups my face, his thumb brushing across my cheek.

"You don't have to do it alone. Whatever happens with us, whatever we figure out—you don't have to be alone."

The words hang between us, heavy with implication. Is he saying what I think he's saying? That he wants to be part of this, part of my future, part of the family I'm trying to build?

"Elliot, we can't—"

"I know. I know it's complicated. I know we have three months and then you're leaving. I know all of that." He leans his forehead against mine. "But I also know that what I feel for you isn't going away. And if you're going to have a baby, if you're going to build a family—I want to be part of it. However that works, whatever that looks like."

My heart is racing, my chest tight with emotions I don't know how to name. This is way beyond what we agreed to. This is him offering me everything I thought I didn't want.

"We should talk about this," I say. "Really talk about it. Not right now, not with your family upstairs, but soon. Because if you're serious—"

"I'm serious."

"Then we need to figure out what that means. What it looks like. How it works with my timeline and your position at Pierce and all the complications we've been ignoring."

"After Christmas," he agrees. "We'll figure it out. But right now—" He kisses me, soft and deep and full of promise. "Right now, I just want to be here with you."

I kiss him back, letting myself believe—just for tonight—that maybe this could work. That maybe we could figure out how to build something real together, despite all the obstacles.

When we finally pull apart, we're both breathing hard.

"I should go to my room," I say reluctantly. "Before your sisters notice we've been out here alone for too long."

"Probably wise." But he doesn't let go. "Cassie, having you here tonight, with my family, felt right. More right than anything has in a long time."

"For me too."

I head inside to my guest room, and he disappears upstairs to the third floor. Separate rooms. Appropriate distance. Playing by the rules.

But lying in bed in the darkness, I can't stop thinking about what he said. That he wants to be part of my future, part of the family I'm building. That whatever we're doing, however complicated it is, he's serious about it.

And I can't stop thinking about dinner tonight—the warmth of his family, the laughter, the sense of belonging I felt sitting at that table. The kind of family I always wanted but convinced myself I could do without.

Maybe I was wrong. Maybe single motherhood isn't the only answer. Maybe there's a version of the future where I get to have the baby I want and the relationship I'm falling into and the family I saw tonight.

Maybe.

But first, we have to get through the next three months without Harrison Gordon finding out. Without jeopardizing Elliot's position. Without the whole thing exploding in our faces.

I fall asleep thinking about possibilities and complications in equal measure, and somewhere in the night I hear a soft knock on my door.

It's Elliot, standing in the hallway in pajama pants and a T-shirt, looking uncertain.

"I couldn't sleep," he says quietly. "Can I... is it okay if I just hold you? Just for a little while?"

I should say no. His sisters are in the house. We need to be careful.

But I pull back the covers and let him climb in beside me, and we fall asleep tangled together, pretending for one night that this is our life—that tomorrow won't bring complications, that three months isn't a deadline, that we have all the time in the world.

13

———

Elliot

KEELEY and her family and Nina leave the day after Christmas and suddenly the house feels different. Quieter. More intimate. Just me and Cassie in this three-story Spanish house that now feels like it belongs to both of us rather than just me.

"Your house is so quiet without the kids," Cassie says on that first morning, standing in the kitchen doorway watching me make coffee. She's wearing my Stanford T-shirt and a pair of pajama pants, her hair still messy from sleep, looking more at home here than I could have imagined a week ago.

"Too quiet?" I ask, handing her a mug.

"No. It's perfect." She takes a sip, then smiles over the rim. "Though I do kind of miss Téa asking me eight hundred questions about everything."

"Give it time. When you see her again, you'll remember why quiet is good."

We end up on the back patio with our coffee, looking out at the terraced garden in the morning light. December in Los Angeles means the garden is in its winter rest period, but there's still work to be done—pruning, clean-up, preparation for spring. I usually have the gardeners only do the basic stuff, leaving most of the planting to me or when my mother was alive, to her.

"Your garden is beautiful," Cassie says, following my gaze to the terraced beds that climb up the hillside behind the house. "Even in winter, you can tell someone put a lot of love into it."

"My mom's garden. I've mostly just been trying to keep it alive since she died, but other than the grass and the hedges, I'm not doing a great job." I set down my mug, studying the overgrown beds with a critical eye. "I planned on working on it during the holiday break but—"

"I could help," Cassie offers quietly. "I'm not an expert, but I helped my mom with her garden growing up. Basic stuff—deadheading, pruning, winter clean-up. If you want."

The offer does something unexpected to my chest. Not just the practical help, but the casual intimacy of it—spending the day working in the yard together, doing the kind of ordinary couple activities we've never had the chance to do. Everything between us has been stolen moments and secret encounters, nothing as mundane and domestic as yard work.

"Yeah," I say, surprised by how much I want this. "I'd really like that."

WE SPEND the morning in the garden, both of us wearing old clothes I dig out of the back of my closet—me in worn jeans and a T-shirt that's seen better days, Cassie swimming in a pair of my sweatpants that she has to roll up at the ankles and one of my old hoodies. She looks ridiculous and beautiful, her hair pulled back in a messy ponytail, dirt already smudged on her cheek from brushing her hair back with dirty hands.

The terraced beds are full of California natives that my mom chose specifically for the climate—drought-tolerant plants that thrive in dry summers and mild winters. Sage, buckwheat, penstemon, all of them needing deadheading and shaping before spring growth starts. Cassie moves through the beds with surprising confidence, showing me which stems to cut, how to shape the plants to encourage healthy growth, explaining the reasoning behind each cut in a way that makes it feel less intimidating.

"My mom loved gardening," she says, kneeling beside an overgrown sage plant and showing me the proper angle for pruning. "She said it was the only thing that kept her sane after my dad left. We had this tiny backyard in San Jose—I mean really tiny, you could probably fit the whole thing in one of your terraces—but she filled every inch of it with plants. Vegetables, flowers, herbs, whatever she could make grow."

"Does she still garden? At the facility in Portland?"

"They have community gardens. She keeps a small plot —mostly herbs and some vegetables. She complains about the clay soil constantly." Cassie sits back on her heels, looking at the trimmed sage in her hands with a small smile. "She'd like your garden. Your mom had good instincts with plant selection. These are all perfect for this climate and exposure."

We work in companionable silence for a while, and there's something meditative about the repetitive motion of trimming and clearing, the sun gradually warming my shoulders as it climbs higher, the distant sounds of the neighborhood going about its Saturday morning routines. Cassie hums softly while she works a few feet away, some melody I don't recognize, and I find myself watching her more than the plants I'm supposed to be pruning.

This is what contentment feels like, I realize. Not the adrenaline rush of closing deals or the satisfaction of successful board presentations, but this—ordinary moments with someone who makes everything feel easier, better, more real.

By early afternoon, we've cleared most of the beds and have accumulated an impressive pile of trimmings for the compost. We're both filthy, sweating despite the mild temperature, with dirt under our fingernails and bits of leaves stuck in our hair. Cassie has a smudge of soil across her forehead and another on her neck, and she's never looked more beautiful to me.

"I desperately need a shower," she announces, standing and stretching with an unselfconscious ease that makes my mouth go dry. "I'm covered in dirt and I'm pretty sure something crawled down my shirt at some point."

"You look beautiful."

"I look like I've been wrestling with your garden and losing." But she's smiling as she says it, that slight upturn of her lips that I've learned means she's pleased despite the protest.

"The garden definitely won," I agree, standing and brushing dirt off my jeans in a futile gesture. "But yeah, we should probably clean up."

She looks at me for a long moment, something shifting in her expression from amused to heated. "We could save water. Shower together."

My heart kicks hard against my ribs. We've been alone in

this house for less than twenty-four hours and we're already abandoning any pretense of separate rooms and appropriate boundaries. "That's very environmentally conscious of you."

"I'm very concerned about conservation." But she's moving closer now, reaching up to brush a leaf out of my hair, her fingers lingering against my temple. "Plus your shower looked really nice when you showed me the master suite yesterday. Big enough for two?"

"Let's find out."

The master bathroom on the third floor is one of the few things I updated after my mom died—replacing her old tub-shower combo with a large walk-in shower with dual rainfall heads and heated tile floors. I turn on the water, adjusting the temperature while Cassie peels off the borrowed sweatpants and hoodie, dropping them in a pile by the door.

"This isn't actually going to save water, you know," she points out, pulling the Stanford T-shirt over her head and adding it to the pile. "We're probably going to use twice as much standing around enjoying the hot water."

"Probably." I'm having significant difficulty focusing on water conservation statistics while she's standing there in just her underwear, dirt smudged on her collarbone, her hair falling loose around her shoulders as she pulls out the ponytail holder. "But I think the environmental benefits are secondary at this point."

"Secondary to what?" She's smiling now, that full smile that transforms her whole face.

"Secondary to getting to see you like this without worrying about someone walking in. Secondary to having all the time we want instead of stealing fifteen minutes in my office." I cross the space between us, running my hands down her arms. "Secondary to the fact that I've been thinking about this all morning while we were working in the garden."

"Have you?" Her hands come up to my chest, fingers working at the buttons of my shirt. "I thought you were very focused on learning proper pruning techniques."

"I was multitasking."

She laughs, and the sound fills the steamy bathroom as the shower continues heating up behind us. We finish undressing each other with increasingly impatient hands, and then we're stepping under the dual sprays, hot water sluicing over both of us, washing away the dirt and sweat from the morning's work.

Cassie tips her head back under one of the rainfall heads, eyes closed, and I just watch for a moment—the water running over her skin, the graceful arch of her neck, the unselfconscious way she moves. She's beautiful in the carefully composed way she presents at work, but this—relaxed, unguarded, completely present—this is devastating.

"You're staring," she says without opening her eyes.

"Can't help it."

"We're supposed to be getting clean." But she's smiling.

"We will." I reach for the shampoo, squeezing some into my palm. "Turn around. Let me wash your hair."

She does, and I work the shampoo through her hair, massaging her scalp, feeling the tension drain out of her shoulders under my hands. This intimacy feels different than sex—more vulnerable somehow, more domestic. Taking care of her, being trusted to touch her like this, the simple pleasure of it without urgency or time pressure bearing down on us.

"That feels amazing," she murmurs, her head falling forward slightly as I work the shampoo through the longer strands.

I rinse it out carefully, making sure to get all the soap, then reach for the body wash. "My turn to get the garden off you."

She turns to face me, water streaming over both of us now, and there's nothing innocent about the way I'm looking at her or the way her breathing has changed. I work the body wash into a lather between my hands and start at her shoulders, working my way down slowly, thoroughly, taking my time learning the geography of her body—every curve, every place that makes her breath catch, every response to my touch.

By the time my soapy hands slide over her hips, we're both breathing harder, the steam and heat making everything feel dreamlike, surreal. She reaches for me, her wet hands sliding over my chest, my shoulders, lower, and I have to brace one hand against the tile wall to stay steady.

She's beautiful, sexy, wet and slick and wanting, and the sight of her naked and aroused makes my pulse kick up, makes me ache for her.

Her hands slide over my wet chest and stomach, her fingers wrapping around me and stroking, and the touch is electric.

"Fuck," I gasp. "Cass, you can't do that."

"I can't?" She sounds amused, and the sound of her voice combined with her touch is almost enough to make me come right then and there.

"We have to—shit, that feels good." She's stroking faster, her grip tighter, and it's all I can do to hold onto some semblance of control. "We have to rinse off first."

She releases me, and I immediately reach for her, pulling her close, kissing her hungrily. "I'm going to taste you."

Her eyes widen slightly, and I can see her pulse flutter in her throat. "Okay."

We rinse off the soap, and then I'm on my knees in front of her, her back pressed against the tile, her legs spread wide to accommodate me. She's dripping wet, and the scent of her is intoxicating.

I start slowly, licking and sucking and tasting, trying to give her time to adjust, but she's already panting, her hips rocking, her fingers tangled in my hair.

"Elliot," she moans. "That feels—so good."

The praise makes me want to give her more, to push her harder. I shift my grip, pressing her against the tile, holding her still as I focus on her clit, sucking and licking and stroking until her whole body is taut, her back arching, her voice high and desperate.

"Please," she begs. "Elliot, please—"

She comes with a sound somewhere between a moan and a scream, her whole body shuddering, her muscles clenching. I stay with her, working her through it, feeling her come apart and listening to her breathing slowly return to normal.

Finally, she reaches down, cupping my face in her hands and drawing me up to kiss her. "You're incredible."

I press my forehead against hers, both of us still panting slightly. "So are you."

She kisses me again, and I can taste her on my tongue, the salt-sweetness of her. "I want you," she whispers, and I'm lost, completely lost.

"Cassie—" Her name comes out rough, ragged, and she wraps her legs around my waist, pulling me closer.

"Bedroom," she whispers. "Now."

We stumble out of the shower, leaving a puddle of water on the floor and a mess of discarded towels, and make it as far as the bed before falling on each other in a tangle of limbs. She's warm and wet and willing, and I'm aching for her, desperate to be inside her.

"Condom," I manage, reaching for my nightstand.

She doesn't argue, just watches me roll the condom on, her eyes hot and hungry, and then she's guiding me into her, her legs wrapping around me, her hands clutching my shoulders.

"Elliot," she gasps as I thrust deeper, her back arching off the bed, her body rising to meet mine.

"Fuck," I groan. "Cass, you feel—"

"So good," she pants. "Don't stop. Don't ever stop."

It's a race toward release, both of us desperate and greedy, her body meeting mine with a slap of flesh, our breathing ragged, our voices loud in the quiet bedroom. Her nails rake down my back, and I can feel the pressure building, the inevitable rush that's about to hit me like a freight train. Two days of not being able to be inside her yet being so close, of touching and kissing and wanting and not having, has me ready to explode.

I'm not going to last. I'm too close, and the way she's moving her hips, the way her muscles are fluttering around me, tells me she's just as close.

"Come for me," I say, and she moans.

"I am, I am—"

She breaks off, her body arching, her eyes slamming shut, and I can feel her orgasm start, can feel her muscles tighten and release, can feel her breathing change. It's too much, the sight and sound and sensation, and I follow her over the edge, coming with a shout, my body shuddering, every nerve alight with the force of it.

We're both still for a moment, panting, spent, our bodies shaking slightly from the intensity of it.

"Fuck," she whispers finally, and I can't help but laugh.

"I'll second that."

She smiles, and the expression is open and relaxed, her lips slightly swollen from the kisses, her cheeks flushed, her eyes heavy-lidded and sated.

I'm looking down at her, and suddenly it feels like a revelation, like something deep inside me has been cracked open, letting light and warmth and possibility flood in.

But I don't tell her. I don't say anything.

I press a kiss to her forehead, her nose, her lips, and let the truth of it settle in.

I'm falling in love with Cassie Reynolds, and the realization is more terrifying than anything else I can remember.

14

Cassie

THE NEXT TWO days blur together in the best possible way, each one building on the one before until they form this perfect bubble of domesticity that I know can't last but desperately want to preserve.

We fall into routines that feel surprisingly natural. Mornings are slow—waking up tangled together in his bed, making coffee we drink on the patio, cooking breakfast together. Elliot runs most mornings while I stay in bed reading, and I love the domesticity of being in his kitchen when he returns, both of us moving around each other with an ease that shouldn't exist yet.

We spend afternoons exploring the neighborhood on foot or hiking the trails that wind up into the hills. The Eagle Rock area is charming in a way I didn't expect—quiet streets, interesting architecture, gardens that make me want to stop and study the plant choices. It's completely different from San Francisco, but I find myself appreciating it more each day.

We cook together most evenings, experimenting in his

kitchen. I talk him through techniques he's uncertain about, and he's surprisingly good at following direction when he's not trying to improvise. We make Filipino dishes from recipes he's clearly made before—pancit, lumpia, adobo that gets better each time we attempt it.

"This is better," I say one evening, tasting our latest batch of adobo. "The vinegar-to-soy ratio is definitely better. Maybe slightly less sugar next time?"

"You think?"

"Definitely. And the chicken is more tender—you're getting better at not overcooking it."

He looks pleased in a way that's endearing, like he's proud of mastering something that matters to him.

We spend an entire afternoon tackling the overgrown bougainvillea threatening to consume the back fence. I show him how to prune properly without killing the plant, and we work side by side in comfortable silence—the kind that doesn't need constant conversation.

"You're good at this," he says, watching me shape a particularly unruly branch.

"My mom taught me." I sit back, surveying the work with satisfaction. "She had strong opinions about pruning—said you have to know when to let things grow wild and when to give them structure."

I think about that sometimes. About what kind of mother I'll be. Whether I'll find the right balance between control and freedom.

"You'll be amazing," Elliot says, and his voice is so sincere it makes my chest tight. "Patient, thoughtful, present. Exactly what any kid would need."

I don't respond, just turn back to the bougainvillea. Because thinking about motherhood means thinking about

April, about leaving, about the future I've planned that doesn't include him. And we're not talking about the future this week.

One afternoon while we're in the garden—me dead-heading the penstemon while Elliot clears clogged drainage channels—I say something that surprises even me.

"I could get used to this." I'm not looking at him, focused on the plant in front of me, but I can feel the weight of the words. "The garden, the cooking, just having time to exist without constantly being pulled in different directions."

The silence stretches for a moment. I can feel him watching me, can almost hear what he wants to say—that I could have this, that we could build something beyond these few stolen days.

But he doesn't push. "We still have a few more days. Let's make the most of them."

I nod, still not looking at him, grateful he didn't force a conversation about the future we're both carefully avoiding.

We go back to our separate tasks, but something has shifted slightly—an acknowledgment that this can't last, that reality is waiting just beyond the edges of this perfect week.

Elliot's still asleep when I wake up on the fourth morning. I watch him for a moment in the early morning light, then carefully slip out of bed and grab his Stanford T-shirt from the floor. It's soft and worn and smells like him, and I pull it on over my underwear before padding downstairs barefoot.

The kitchen is bright with morning sunlight. I move through it with the ease of someone who's spent the past four days learning where everything is—coffee in the upper cabinet, mugs by the sink, eggs in the refrigerator. I start the coffee maker and pull out ingredients for breakfast. Eggs, bread for toast, the strawberries we bought at the farmers market yesterday.

I'm whisking eggs when I hear the front door open.

My heart jumps. Elliot's still asleep upstairs, and no one else should have a key to his house. I freeze, the whisk still in my hand, as footsteps move through the entryway toward the kitchen.

Then Declan's voice: "Elliot? You home?"

Oh god.

I look down at myself—wearing nothing but Elliot's T-shirt and underwear, standing in his kitchen making breakfast, very obviously having spent the night. There's no way to hide this, no explanation that makes this look like anything other than what it is.

Declan appears in the kitchen doorway, Maya right behind him. They both stop dead when they see me.

The silence stretches for approximately three seconds that feel like three hours.

"Well," Maya finally says, her expression shifting from surprise to something that looks almost like satisfaction. "This explains why he's been so sparse with his texts."

Before anyone can say anything else, I hear footsteps on the stairs.

"Declan?" Elliot's voice carries from the hallway, and then he's appearing in the kitchen doorway, barefoot, wearing pajama pants and no shirt, his hair sticking up in every direction. He stops when he sees all of us, and something like resignation mixed with relief crosses his face.

"Hey," he says, moving into the kitchen to stand next to me, his hand finding the small of my back. "I heard the door. Thought it might be you."

"You heard the door but didn't think to text me back all week?" Declan says, but there's no heat in it—just mild exasperation and maybe amusement. "Maya's been ready to file a missing person report."

"I texted you back. Told you I was fine."

"One text. Very reassuring." Declan's eyes move between Elliot and me, and a slow smile spreads across his face. "Though I see now why you've been unavailable."

"Declan, Maya—this is Cassie Reynolds," Elliot says. "Cassie, this is Declan Pierce and Maya Navarro."

"We've heard about you," Maya says warmly, stepping forward with an extended hand. "Elliot's compliance officer from Pierce."

I shake her hand, acutely aware that I'm doing this while wearing only Elliot's T-shirt. "That's me. Sorry about the, um —" I gesture vaguely at my state of undress.

"Don't apologize," Maya says, smiling. "We're the ones who showed up unannounced."

"I've been texting him all week," Declan explains, though he doesn't seem upset about it. "When he went radio silent, we got worried. Figured we'd do a wellness check."

"Well, he's clearly alive," Maya says, her tone light and teasing. "And apparently doing very well."

Elliot's hand is still on my back, warm and steady. "Sorry I worried you. I just needed some time to disconnect."

"Clearly," Declan says, but he's smiling now. "We won't stay long. Just wanted to make sure you hadn't been kidnapped or—" He stops, seeming to realize this is getting awkward. "Anyway. You're fine. That's what matters."

"Actually," Maya says, glancing at the bowl of whisked eggs and the ingredients spread across the counter, "it smells like you were making breakfast. We don't want to interrupt—"

"You're not interrupting," I hear myself say, even though part of me desperately wants them to leave so I can process this mortifying situation in private. "I was just making scrambled eggs and toast. There's plenty if you want to stay."

The words come out before I've fully thought them through, but once they're out there, I realize I mean them. These are Elliot's family and close friends. If we're going to keep this relationship secret from everyone at Pierce, at least we don't have to hide from the people who actually matter to him.

"We don't want to impose," Declan starts, but Maya's already moving toward the table.

"We'd love to stay," she says firmly, giving Declan a look that suggests this isn't up for debate. "Thank you, Cassie. Can I help with anything?"

"You could set the table?" I gesture toward the cabinets. "Plates are up there, silverware in the drawer by the sink."

Maya moves with easy familiarity through Elliot's kitchen, clearly comfortable here from previous visits, and starts pulling out plates and mugs. Declan watches this domestic scene with an expression I can't quite read—surprise, maybe, or amusement, or something more thoughtful.

"I should put on actual clothes," I say, suddenly very aware that I'm still wearing only Elliot's T-shirt. "If you'll excuse me for a minute—"

"Take your time," Maya says warmly as I escape upstairs, my heart racing.

This is not how I imagined this morning going. I'd planned to make breakfast, spend a quiet last day with Elliot, maybe talk about how we're going to handle going back to work in two days. Not have an impromptu breakfast party with the former CEO of Pierce Enterprises and the girlfriend he gave up his position for while wearing the current CEO's shirt like some kind of cliché.

In Elliot's bedroom, I find my jeans from yesterday and pull them on, then grab one of my own sweaters from the small bag I brought. I run my fingers through my hair, trying to make it look less like I just rolled out of bed, and take a moment to breathe.

I can do this. I can have breakfast with my secret boyfriend's family and act like a normal person instead of someone who's been caught in a compromising position.

When I come back downstairs, Elliot's put on a T-shirt and is pouring coffee while Declan leans against the counter and Maya finishes setting the table. They all look up when I enter, and I feel absurdly self-conscious in my own clothes.

"Better?" I ask, gesturing to my outfit.

"You looked fine before," Maya says kindly. "But I imagine this feels less awkward."

"Significantly less awkward," I admit, moving back to the stove to finish the eggs. "Though I apologize for the whole situation. This probably wasn't how you expected your wellness check to go."

"We've had stranger mornings," Declan says, accepting a mug of coffee from Elliot. "Remember that time we showed up at your apartment in college and you were hosting an impromptu study group in your pajamas?"

"That was one time," Elliot protests. "And it was finals week."

"You were teaching a seminar on corporate finance theory while wearing SpongeBob boxers."

Maya laughs. "I would have paid to see that."

The tension in the room eases slightly with the banter, and I focus on cooking the eggs, grateful for something to do with my hands. Behind me, I can hear Elliot and Declan talking quietly, their voices low enough that I can't make out the words, and Maya appears at my elbow.

"Can I help with anything?" she asks.

"Could you grab the bread? It's in the pantry, left side." I gesture with the spatula. "And there's butter in the fridge if you want to start the toast."

We work side by side for a few minutes, and Maya's presence is surprisingly calming. She doesn't pry or ask awkward questions, just helps with breakfast like this is a normal morning and she's a normal guest rather than someone who just caught me in a compromising position with her fiancé's cousin.

"I know this must be incredibly awkward," Maya says quietly, dropping bread into the toaster. "But Declan and I aren't going to make it weird or tell anyone. Your secret's safe with us."

"Thank you," I say, meaning it. "I know it looks—I mean, this probably seems reckless or—"

"It looks like two people who care about each other spending time together." Maya's voice is gentle. "That's not something to apologize for."

"Even when one of those people is supposed to be providing independent compliance oversight of the other?"

"Especially then. Life's complicated. Relationships don't follow neat professional boundaries." She pulls plates from the warming drawer. "Declan and I met when he was CEO of Pierce and I was running Highland Community Center.

There were complications there too—power dynamics, professional conflicts, all of it. We figured it out."

"How did you handle it?"

"Honestly? We tried to fight it for a while. Pretended it was just professional. That worked exactly as well as you'd expect." She smiles. "Eventually we admitted what was happening and dealt with the complications as they came up. It wasn't easy, but it was worth it."

The eggs are done, and I turn off the heat, spooning them onto a serving platter. "Did people judge you? Question whether your relationship compromised your work?"

"Some people did. Harrison Gordon especially—he tried to use it against Declan, claimed his judgment was compromised." Maya's expression hardens slightly. "But Declan didn't let that change his decisions. He chose what mattered to him and dealt with the fallout."

I want to ask more—want to know how they navigated the professional complications, how they dealt with the scrutiny, whether she ever regretted the choice. But Declan and Elliot are moving back toward the kitchen, and the moment for private conversation passes.

"Breakfast is ready," I announce, carrying the platter of eggs to the table.

We settle around the dining table—the same one where I ate Christmas Eve dinner with Elliot's family just a few days ago—and for a few minutes there's just the comfortable sounds of people eating breakfast together.

"So," Declan says eventually, setting down his fork. "I have to ask—how long has this been going on?"

Elliot and I exchange a glance.

"Depends on how you define 'this,'" Elliot says carefully.

"We've known each other for seven years—I was her student at Stanford, remember?"

"And the relationship part?" Declan's tone is curious rather than accusatory, but there's an edge of concern underneath.

"San Diego," I reply, "Mid-December. That's when things... shifted."

"So about two weeks." Declan processes this. "And you're keeping it completely secret at Pierce?"

"We have to," I say firmly. "Harrison is already watching for any sign that my compliance assessment is biased. If he finds out Elliot and I are involved, he'll use it to undermine both of us."

"He would," Maya agrees. "Harrison's looking for any excuse to question Elliot's leadership."

"Which is why no one at Pierce can know," Elliot adds. "Not the board, not Colton, not anyone. At least not until Cassie's contract ends in March."

"And then what?" Declan asks. "She leaves and you just... what? Keep seeing each other long-distance? Hope no one at Pierce connects the dots?"

It's a fair question, and one I don't have a good answer for. Elliot and I haven't talked about what happens after my contract ends, haven't discussed how this relationship fits with my fertility plans or his position at Pierce or any of the long-term logistics that make this complicated.

"We're figuring it out," Elliot says, which is both true and completely inadequate.

Declan looks like he wants to say more, but Maya touches his hand gently. "Maybe this is a conversation you and Elliot should have privately?"

"Yeah." Declan stands, picking up his coffee mug. "Walk,

you want to show me whatever you've been doing with the back garden? I heard you've been actually maintaining it for once."

Elliot glances at me, a silent question in his eyes. I nod slightly—they should talk, and I should probably have a conversation with Maya without the guys hovering.

"Sure," Elliot says, standing. "We've been doing some winter clean-up. Cassie's been teaching me how not to kill everything my mom planted."

The two of them head out to the patio, sliding the glass door closed behind them, and suddenly it's just Maya and me at the dining table with half-finished breakfast between us.

"Sorry about that," Maya says. "Declan worries. It's what he does."

"He's right to worry. This is risky." I take a sip of coffee, trying to organize my thoughts. "I know how it looks—the compliance officer sleeping with the CEO she's supposed to be monitoring. It's a massive conflict of interest."

"Is it though?" Maya's watching me thoughtfully. "From what Elliot's told Declan, your work at Pierce is exemplary. You're thorough, objective, exactly what they hired you to be. Your personal relationship doesn't change that."

"Harrison Gordon will say it does."

"Harrison Gordon is a manipulative bastard who's been trying to undermine Elliot since before he even became CEO." Maya's voice is matter-of-fact. "He'll find something to criticize regardless. At least this way you're living your life instead of making decisions based on what Harrison might think."

I want to believe that. Want to think that my professional integrity speaks for itself, that my relationship with Elliot doesn't compromise my work, that we can navigate this without it blowing up in both our faces.

But I've spent twenty years in corporate compliance. I know how these things look from the outside. I know how easily perception becomes reality in the eyes of a board looking for reasons to question leadership.

"How did you deal with it?" I ask. "When people questioned your relationship with Declan—how did you handle the scrutiny?"

"Honestly? It was hard. There were people at Pierce who thought I was using Declan for Highland's benefit, and people at Highland who thought I was selling out to corporate interests." Maya traces the rim of her coffee mug. "But the people who mattered—the people who actually knew us —they saw that we were both trying to do the right thing. That we could be in a relationship and still maintain our professional integrity."

"And the people who didn't believe that?"

"We proved them wrong. With time and consistency and by not letting their doubts change how we operated." She pauses. "Look, I'm not going to tell you this is easy. It's not. Keeping your relationship secret while working together, navigating the professional complications, dealing with people like Harrison who will absolutely use it against you —it's all hard. But if Elliot is worth it to you, then you figure it out."

Is he worth it? That's the question, isn't it. Is what I feel for Elliot worth the professional risk, the scrutiny, the complications? Worth potentially derailing my carefully planned timeline for motherhood? Worth upending the life I've constructed specifically to avoid this kind of messy, complicated entanglement?

Through the patio doors, I can see Elliot and Declan talking, their body language serious but not confrontational. Elliot gestures toward the terraced garden, explaining something, and even from here I can see the way his whole demeanor changes when he talks about the work we've done together this week.

"I don't know," I admit quietly. "I care about him. A lot. But this situation—keeping it secret, navigating the professional complications—it's a lot to manage."

"It is," Maya agrees. "But from what I've seen this morning, it seems like you two have something real. That's worth fighting for."

I want to believe her. Want to think that what Elliot and I have can survive the scrutiny and complications waiting for us at Pierce.

But I've spent my whole adult life making careful, rational decisions specifically to avoid this kind of uncertainty.

"I should probably get going soon," I say, changing the subject before it gets too heavy. "I need to head back to my apartment today, get ready for returning to work on Thursday."

"You're not staying through New Year's?"

"I think it's better if I don't. We've had three days of—" I search for the right word. "—pretending this is normal. But it's not normal, and we both need to remember that before we go back to Pierce."

Maya nods slowly. "That's probably smart. Though you're welcome at our place for New Year's Eve if you don't want to spend it alone. We're having people over—nothing fancy, just friends and food."

The invitation surprises me. "That's really kind, but—"

"Think about it. The offer stands." She stands, collecting empty plates. "I'm going to start cleaning up. You relax."

"You're a guest. I should—"

"You cooked. I clean. That's the rule." She's already moving toward the kitchen, but I follow anyway, needing to do something with my hands.

We work together washing dishes and putting away leftovers, and the conversation shifts to easier topics—her work at Highland, my previous jobs, mutual complaints about LA traffic. By the time Declan and Elliot come back inside, the kitchen is clean and Maya and I are laughing about a disastrous compliance audit I conducted years ago that involved three different departments all blaming each other for the same policy violation.

"Everything okay out there?" I ask Elliot as he slides the patio door closed.

"Yeah. Just catching up." He glances at Declan. "We should probably let you two get on with your day."

"Right. Yeah." Declan moves toward the entryway, Maya following. "Thanks for breakfast, Cassie. It was really nice to meet you."

"You too. Both of you."

At the door, Maya pulls me into a quick hug. "Remember—New Year's Eve, our place, if you want company. I'll text you the address."

"Thank you."

After they leave, Elliot and I stand in the suddenly quiet house, the weight of reality settling back over us.

"Well," I say finally. "That was unexpected."

"But good, I think. They liked you."

"Declan seemed worried."

"Declan's always worried. It's his default state." Elliot

pulls me closer. "But he's not going to say anything. Neither is Maya. We're safe."

Safe. It's a relative term, I think. We're safe from Declan and Maya telling anyone, but we're not safe from the inherent risks of what we're doing. We're not safe from Harrison finding out some other way. We're not safe from the complications that are inevitably coming.

"I should pack," I say quietly. "I need to get back to my apartment today."

"You're leaving?" He sounds surprised, maybe hurt.

"We go back to work in two days, Elliot. I need time to… regroup. Ground myself. Remember who I am outside of this bubble we've been in."

"You could stay through New Year's."

"I could. But I don't think that's smart." I pull back to look at him. "These three days have been perfect. But we need to be realistic about what we're walking back into. Harrison watching our every interaction. The board expecting my independent assessment. All the professional complications we've been ignoring."

He's quiet for a moment, then nods. "You're right. You're absolutely right."

We spend the rest of the morning in a strange kind of limbo—both of us aware that this perfect bubble is ending, neither of us quite ready to acknowledge it fully. I pack my bag slowly, making sure I have everything, and when I come downstairs Elliot's made sandwiches for lunch.

We eat on the patio one last time, and the conversation is lighter than the morning's intensity—plans for New Year's Eve (him at Maya and Declan's, me probably at home), whether we'll see each other before Thursday (probably not, safer that way), how we'll handle seeing each other at the office (very carefully).

By two PM, I'm standing by my car with my bag, and Elliot's walked me out like this is a normal goodbye instead of the end of three days that felt like a different life entirely.

"Thank you," I say. "For inviting me. For Christmas with your family, for this week—all of it."

"Thank you for saying yes." He cups my face, kissing me softly. "I'll see you at work."

"Back to being professionals."

"Right. Professionals." But he's smiling slightly. "Who happen to care about each other."

"That sounds like a disaster waiting to happen."

"Probably," he says. "But I've never been good at playing it safe."

I kiss him one more time, then get in my car before I can change my mind about leaving. As I drive away, I watch him in the rearview mirror standing in front of his house, and something in my chest aches.

Five days. That's all we had of pretending this could work, of living like we weren't walking a professional tightrope that could snap at any moment.

Now we're going back to reality.

And I have no idea if what we built in that house can survive it.

15

Elliot

THE FIRST DAY back at Pierce feels surreal after the week at my house with Cassie.

Actually, it's torture.

I saw her briefly this morning when she arrived—she was walking toward her office, I was coming out of mine, and our eyes met for just a second before she looked away and kept walking. Professional. Distant. Exactly what we agreed we needed to be at the office.

It's killing me.

My phone buzzes with a text from Colton about needing to review last quarter projections. I text my reply and set down my phone, forcing myself to focus on the emails.

End-of-year reports from various departments. Updates on the Blaisdell merger integration timeline. A meeting request from Harrison Gordon for later this week that I accept with reluctance because ignoring him would be more suspicious than meeting with him.

My office door is open, and I can hear the usual sounds of the executive floor coming back to life after the holiday break—phones ringing, voices in the hallway, the elevator chiming as people come and go. Everything is normal. Everything is exactly as it should be.

Except I keep glancing toward Cassie's office, hoping to catch another glimpse of her, and having to force myself to look away before anyone notices.

By lunchtime, I've managed to make it through several hours of work without doing anything stupid like walking past Cassie's office for no reason or finding an excuse to talk to her. I'm calling this a victory, even though it feels like failure.

Like running into Harrison Gordon in the hallway.

"Elliot," he says, his tone pleasant in that way that always makes me wary. "Welcome back. How was your holiday?"

"Good. Quiet. Spent it with family." All true, though I'm very carefully not mentioning which family or who else might have been there.

"That's nice. It's important to disconnect during the holidays." Harrison falls into step beside me as we walk toward the elevator. "I tried calling you a few times over the break. Some questions about the Blaisdell timeline."

My stomach drops. He called? I'd had my phone silenced most of the week, barely checking it except for Declan's increasingly worried texts. If Harrison called and I didn't answer, did that raise flags?

"Sorry about that. I was really trying to unplug for a few days." I keep my voice casual. "What did you need regarding Blaisdell?"

"Oh, nothing urgent. I was just curious about the integration timeline Colton proposed." We step into the elevator together, and Harrison presses the button for the lobby. "You know me—always thinking ahead about potential complications."

Always looking for problems, more like. Always trying to find angles to question my decisions or undermine my authority. But I just nod. "The timeline is solid. Cassie's compliance review flagged some areas that need work, but nothing that changes the fundamental deal."

"Ah yes. Ms. Reynolds." Harrison's tone is still pleasant, but something shifts slightly. "How is her assessment going?"

"Well. She's thorough." I'm being very careful with my words, very aware that any hint of familiarity could be dangerous. "Her preliminary findings are due mid-February."

"And you're satisfied with her work? No concerns about objectivity or thoroughness?"

The question feels loaded, like he's fishing for something. "No concerns at all. She's exactly what we hired her to be—independent and exacting."

"Good. That's good." The elevator reaches the lobby, and Harrison steps out. "Well, enjoy your lunch. We should catch up properly sometime this week. Compare notes on Q4."

"Sure. I'll have my assistant set something up."

I watch him walk away toward the main entrance, and something about the conversation sits wrong with me. The way he asked about Cassie. The way he mentioned trying to call me during the break. The casual tone that felt anything but casual.

Does he know something? Did someone see us together? Is he fishing, or does he actually have information?

I head to the café down the street on autopilot, my mind replaying the conversation, looking for hidden meaning in every word. Harrison's too smart to make direct accusations without evidence, but he's excellent at planting seeds of doubt, making people second-guess themselves.

And it's working. Because now I'm wondering if we were careful enough over the holidays. If someone saw us at the farmers market or hiking in Eagle Rock. If a neighbor mentioned seeing a woman at my house. If Declan or Maya said something to someone who said something to someone else.

I'm spiraling, and I know it. But I can't seem to stop.

THE AFTERNOON MEETING with Colton is a welcome distraction. We spend two hours going through Q4 numbers and preparing for Tuesday's board presentation, and for those two hours I manage to focus on something other than Harrison's loaded questions and whether my relationship with Cassie is about to blow up in both our faces.

"These projections are strong," Colton says, closing his laptop. "The board should be pleased. Especially with the Blaisdell integration timeline looking solid."

"Cassie's compliance review helped with that. Her recommendations are going to make integration smoother."

"She's good. Really good." Colton studies me for a moment. "You seem tense, though. Everything okay?"

"Fine. Just first-day-back stress."

"Right." He doesn't look convinced, but he doesn't push. "Well, if you need anything before Tuesday's meeting, let me know."

After Colton leaves, I sit in the empty conference room trying to talk myself down from the ledge I'm on. Harrison asking questions doesn't mean he knows anything. It just means he's Harrison—suspicious, strategic, always looking for leverage. I'm reading too much into a casual conversation because I'm paranoid about getting caught.

I need to get a grip.

I head back to my office, determined to focus on work for the rest of the afternoon, to stop obsessing over whether Harrison knows something or if I'm just being paranoid.

But when I pass Cassie's office, her door is open, and I can see her at her desk reviewing documents. She looks up as I walk by, and our eyes meet for just a second—just long enough for me to see the same careful distance she's been maintaining all day, the same professional mask we both agreed to wear.

And I hate it. I hate pretending she's just another colleague. I hate walking past her office without stopping. I hate that we're in the same building and I can't touch her or talk to her or even look at her without worrying about who might notice.

I keep walking to my office and close the door.

This is what we signed up for, I remind myself. This is the necessary cost of keeping the relationship secret. We knew it would be hard. We knew we'd have to maintain distance at work.

I just didn't realize how much it would hurt.

By Friday afternoon, I've successfully made it through two full days back at work without doing anything stupid. I've kept appropriate distance from Cassie. I've been professional in the one brief interaction we had during a meeting about the Blaisdell compliance timeline. I've avoided her office except when absolutely necessary.

I've also been miserable, but that's beside the point.

I'm packing up to leave for the day when my phone buzzes with a text from Cassie.

Working late tonight. Lots to catch up on after the break.

It's innocuous. Professional. The kind of message any colleague might send.

But I know what it means. What it's really saying: I'll be here. Alone. If you want to see me.

I should go home. Should maintain the distance we've been keeping. Should remember that Harrison's already asking questions and the last thing we need is to give him ammunition by being careless.

But I don't want to be smart anymore. I don't want to be careful or strategic or professionally appropriate.

I want to see Cassie.

I text back: *Me too. See you around.*

I GIVE IT AN HOUR. Let most of the executive floor clear out, let the building quiet down for the weekend. By seven PM, the floor is nearly empty—just a few scattered offices still lit, most people having left early on a Friday after the holiday break.

Cassie's light is still on.

I should knock. Should announce myself professionally. Should maintain at least the appearance of appropriate boundaries.

Instead I just walk in and close the door behind me.

She looks up from her laptop, and I see surprise flash across her face, followed by something warmer. "Elliot. Hi."

"Hi." I lean against the closed door, just looking at her. "I know we said we'd be careful. I know we agreed to maintain distance at work."

"We did."

"I'm terrible at it." I cross to her desk. "These past two days have been torture. Seeing you and not being able to touch you. Walking past your office and having to pretend you're just another colleague."

"Elliot—"

"I know. I know all the reasons we have to be careful. Harrison's already asking questions—asked about my holiday, about you, about your assessment. I don't know if he knows something or if he's just fishing, but either way it's dangerous." I'm standing in front of her desk now, close enough to touch but not quite touching. "And I don't care. I should care. I should be smart about this. But all I can think about is how much I miss you."

She stands, moving around her desk to stand in front of me. "What did Harrison say exactly?"

"Asked about my holiday. Mentioned he tried calling me during the break and I didn't answer. Asked about your assessment and whether I had concerns about your objectivity." I run a hand through my hair. "It felt loaded. Like he was fishing for something."

"Or he's just being Harrison. Suspicious and strategic about everything."

"Maybe." I reach out, finally letting myself touch her— just my hand on her arm, but even that small contact after two days of distance feels significant. "But it made me realize how exposed we are. How much we're risking."

"Are you having second thoughts?" Her voice is carefully neutral, but I can see the concern in her eyes.

"No. That's the problem." I pull her closer. "I should be. I should be thinking about my career and your reputation and all the professional complications. Instead all I could think about today was how much I wanted to see you. How much I hated pretending."

"We have to pretend. At least here, at work."

"I know. But not tonight." I cup her face. "Tonight I just want to be with you. No pretending, no professional distance. Just us."

She looks at me for a long moment, and I can see her weighing the same risks I've been obsessing over all day. Then she leans up and kisses me, and all the careful distance we've been maintaining dissolves.

We break apart after a moment, both breathing harder.

"We can't do this here," she says. "Not in my office. Too risky."

"My place or yours?"

"Mine. Your place feels too exposed after Declan and Maya walked in."

"Fair point." I step back, trying to regain some composure. "You go first. I'll leave in fifteen minutes. Less suspicious if we're not seen leaving together."

"Okay." She's already gathering her things, shutting down her laptop. "Elliot?"

"Yeah?"

"I missed you too. These past two days. I know we agreed to be professional, but it's been really hard."

"We'll figure it out. How to balance this with work. How to be careful without going crazy." I kiss her again, quick and soft. "But tonight we don't worry about any of that."

She leaves first, and I wait in her office watching the clock. Fifteen minutes feels like an eternity, but I force myself to wait, to be smart about at least this much.

When I finally leave, the executive floor is dark except for the emergency lights. I take the elevator down to the parking garage, and my mind is already racing ahead—to Cassie's apartment, to having her to myself for a night, to temporarily forgetting about Harrison's questions and professional complications and all the reasons this should scare me more than it does.

Harrison's questions planted doubt. Made me question what I'm doing, why I'm risking everything for this relationship.

But one look at Cassie, one touch, and all that doubt evaporates. Because whatever we're risking, whatever complications we're creating—she's worth it.

I just hope we're being careful enough that we don't both pay the price.

Cassie's apartment is in Santa Monica, a half-hour drive from Pierce in light traffic. It's a modern building with secured entry and underground parking—anonymous in a way that makes me grateful. Less chance of being seen here than at my house in Eagle Rock where neighbors know me.

She buzzes me up, and when she opens her door, she's changed out of her work clothes into yoga pants and a soft sweater. Her hair is down, and she's barefoot, and she looks more like the woman I spent Christmas week with than the professional Chief Compliance Officer I've been carefully not looking at for two days.

"Hi," she says, stepping aside to let me in.

"Hi." I close the door behind me and pull her into my arms, finally—finally—able to touch her without worrying about who might see. "God, I've missed this."

"It's been two days."

"Longest two days of my life." I'm kissing her now,

making up for the distance we've had to maintain, and she's kissing me back with the same desperation.

We end up on the couch, her straddling me, my hands under her sweater, my mouth on hers. It feels so good, so right, like we fit together in a way that can't be forced or faked or sustained through pretense.

After a while, she shifts, sitting up and pulling her sweater over her head, leaving her in just her bra.

My mouth goes dry. She really is beautiful—her hair falling loose around her shoulders, her skin pale and smooth, the curves of her body inviting and familiar.

I cup her face, pulling her down for a kiss. "Cassie, you are—God, you are incredible."

"So are you."

She reaches between us, unfastening my pants, and I can feel the urgency in her movements, the heat of her rising off her skin.

"I want you," she whispers against my lips before sliding down between my legs, helping me slide off my pants and boxer briefs. "I need you, Elliot."

"I need you too. So much."

She's on her knees in front of me, and she's working her way up, her mouth finding the inside of my thighs, my hip, the flat plane of my stomach, then finally the sensitive spot at the base of my cock. Her tongue swirls, her fingers dig into my skin, and I can't breathe, can't think, can only feel.

"Cassie—"

"I want to taste you." She looks up, her eyes hooded and heavy. "Can I?"

"Fuck, yes."

She takes me in her mouth, her lips wrapped around me, her cheeks hollowed, and the sight of her on her knees, her mouth working me, is so hot I'm ready to come after just a few seconds.

"Stop." My voice is hoarse. "I can't—not yet."

She releases me, her lips wet and swollen. "You can. You can, Elliot."

She's stroking me, her grip tight, and the combination of her mouth and her hands is too much.

"Cassie," I manage. "God, please, I'm going to—"

She's not stopping, not slowing, and it's too much, too good. My hips jerk, my hands tangle in her hair, and then I'm coming, heat rushing through me, every muscle tight, the force of it stealing my breath.

After a moment, she sits up, wiping her mouth and smiling. "Good?"

"Amazing." I reach for her, pulling her onto the couch and kissing her, tasting myself on her lips. "Let me make you feel good."

"I just did."

"More." I'm pulling her sweatpants and underwear down, my hands running over her body, and she's wet and ready, her legs parting for me. "God, Cassie, you're so fucking sexy."

She doesn't respond. Just gasps as I slide a finger into her, then two, and find the spot that makes her whole body tighten.

"Right there," she manages, her hips moving, her voice high and desperate. "Please, Elliot, just—"

I give her what she needs, my thumb on her clit, my fingers stroking her until she's arching off the couch, her nails digging into my back, her voice rising as she comes apart.

After, we're tangled together on the couch, both still

mostly dressed, the heat and intensity of the past few minutes slowly dissipating.

"Well, that was a hell of a way to start the weekend," I say, pressing a kiss to her shoulder.

She laughs. "It was. And I'm not done with you yet."

"Good, because I'm not done with you either." I stroke her hair, her skin, her body still pressed against mine. "Ready for round two?"

We barely make it to the bedroom.

Afterward, lying tangled together in her bed, I tell her about the full conversation with Harrison—every word I can remember, every loaded question, every moment that made me wonder if he knows something.

"He's fishing," Cassie says, her head on my chest. "Harrison's smart enough to know that direct accusations without evidence would backfire. So he asks questions, plants seeds of doubt, watches to see how people react."

"So you don't think he actually knows?"

"I think if he knew something concrete, he'd use it. The fact that he's still asking questions suggests he's suspicious but doesn't have proof." She traces patterns on my chest. "But we need to be more careful. No more showing up at each other's offices after hours. No more texting anything that could be misconstrued if someone saw our phones."

"I know. You're right." I tighten my arms around her. "But I'm not good at being careful when it comes to you."

"You're going to have to learn. We both are." She lifts her head to look at me. "Because if Harrison finds out, he will use it to destroy us both. Your credibility as CEO, my reputation as an objective compliance officer—everything we've both worked for."

"I know." I do know. I've been telling myself the same

thing for two days. "But being here with you—it makes all that risk feel worth it."

"Even if it costs you the CEO position?"

The question is serious, and I take a moment to really consider it. Would I give up being CEO for Cassie? Would I choose this relationship over the career I've been building toward my entire adult life?

"I don't know," I admit honestly. "I hope I never have to make that choice. But I know I don't want to give you up. Not yet. Not when we're just figuring out what this is."

She's quiet for a moment, and I can feel her pulling back slightly—not physically, but emotionally. Building walls I can sense even in the darkness.

"What are you thinking?" I ask.

"That we should probably be more careful. Not just at work, but... in general." Her voice is measured, controlled. "The less we plan, the less we talk about anything beyond right now, the safer we both are."

"Cassie—"

"I'm serious, Elliot. Every conversation about the future is a risk. Every plan we make together is something that could be used against us if Harrison finds out." She lifts her head to look at me. "So maybe we just... don't. Don't talk about March, don't talk about what happens after, don't make this more complicated than it already is."

There's something in her voice—a defensiveness, maybe, or self-protection. Like she's already preparing for this to end, already building distance even while lying in my arms.

"So we just take it day by day? No conversations about where this is going?"

"Exactly. Day by day. Moment by moment. Isn't that what we agreed? To live in the present?"

It is what we agreed. But something about the way she's saying it now feels different—less like choosing to be present and more like refusing to acknowledge a future we're both afraid to examine too closely.

"Okay," I say finally. "Day by day."

She settles back against my chest, and I try not to think about what she's not saying—that she's protecting herself, protecting me, protecting us both from getting too invested in something that has an expiration date stamped all over it.

We lie there in the darkness, and I try to focus on the present moment—the warmth of her against me, the quiet of her apartment, the simple fact that we're together despite all the risks.

But the doubts are there now. Planted by Harrison's questions and Cassie's careful distance and the growing awareness that we're both walking toward something neither of us is willing to name.

For tonight, though, I'm choosing to ignore them.

For tonight, this is enough.

16

Cassie

I WAKE up on Saturday morning with Elliot's arm draped over my waist, sunlight filtering through my bedroom curtains, and for a moment everything is perfect.

We fell asleep tangled together after he showed up at my apartment last night, after we made love with an urgency that felt like we were both trying to prove something—that we could handle the risk, that being together was worth the complications, that whatever doubts Harrison planted didn't matter as much as this connection between us.

I watch him sleep for a moment, his face relaxed in a way it never is at the office, and something in my chest aches. I've never felt this way about anyone. Not Brad, despite five years together. Not anyone in the handful of relationships I had before him. This thing with Elliot is different—deeper, more consuming, more terrifying because of how much I have to lose.

He stirs, his eyes opening slowly, and when he sees me watching him, he smiles. "Morning."

"Morning." I lean in to kiss him, soft and sweet. "Coffee?"

"Please."

We get up and I make coffee while he showers, and by the time he emerges—hair damp, wearing yesterday's clothes—I have two mugs ready and am contemplating whether I have anything in my refrigerator that constitutes breakfast.

"I should probably go," he says, accepting the coffee. "Get home, change, be a responsible adult." He pauses, looking around my apartment with a small smile. "Though I have to say, I like waking up at my girlfriend's place."

Girlfriend. He's never used that word before, and it hangs in the air between us—significant, weighted with implications we've been avoiding.

"Probably wise," I say, even though I don't want him to leave. "We're being reckless enough as it is."

He sets down his mug and pulls me close. "Worth it though."

"Is it?" The question comes out before I can stop it. "Elliot, what are we doing? Really? We can't keep this up forever. We should be more careful."

He kisses the top of my head. "We will be. Starting Monday."

He leaves around nine, and I walk him to the door, both of us lingering in that awkward goodbye space where we're not quite ready to separate but know we should.

"I'll text you later," he says.

"Okay."

He kisses me one more time and heads down the hallway. I close the door and lean against it for a moment, smiling despite myself before heading to the kitchen to clean up our coffee mugs.

I'm rinsing them in the sink when my phone rings fifteen minutes later. Elliot.

"Miss me already?" I answer, smiling.

"I ran into someone." His voice is tight, serious. "In the parking garage. Kevin from IT."

My stomach drops. "What?"

"He was getting into his car when I was leaving. Asked what I was doing here."

"What did you tell him?"

"That I was dropping off your laptop—that you'd forgotten it at the office Friday and needed it for urgent compliance documents over the weekend." He pauses. "I know it's flimsy, but it was the first thing I could think of."

I glance at my laptop sitting on the dining table. "My laptop."

"I know. But if anyone asks, that's the story. You forgot your laptop Friday, I was nearby this morning, I dropped it off. Can you back that up?"

"Yes. Of course." My mind is already racing through the implications. Kevin from IT saw Elliot leaving my building at nine AM on a Saturday, still wearing what he wore yesterday to work. That's not proof of anything, but it's suspicious. And if Kevin mentions it to anyone, if it gets back to Harrison—

"Cassie, it's going to be fine," Elliot says, as if reading my silence. "Kevin's not a gossip, not political. He probably won't mention it to anyone."

"You don't know that."

"No, but I know Kevin. He minds his own business. And even if he does say something, we have a plausible explanation." His voice softens. "We're going to be okay. Just stick to the story if anyone asks."

"Okay." But my heart is racing.

"I'm sorry. I should have been more careful, should have checked the garage before—"

"It's not your fault. We knew there was risk." I press my hand to my forehead. "We just got unlucky."

After we hang up, I stand in my kitchen staring at my laptop, the worry sitting heavy in my stomach.

This is fine. Kevin probably won't say anything. And even if he does, we have an explanation. Dropping off a laptop isn't evidence of a relationship. It's just a colleague helping another colleague.

But the worry doesn't go away. It sits there all weekend, turning every time I think about it.

HARRISON GORDON SHOWS up at my office door Monday morning while I'm looking over operations procedures.

"Harrison. Good morning." I keep my voice professional, neutral even as my body goes on full alert. "What can I do for you?"

"Just checking in," he says, stepping into my office uninvited, his hands in his trouser pockets. "Wanted to see how the assessment is progressing. The board is very eager for your preliminary findings."

"It's going well. I'm on track to have draft findings ready by mid-February as planned."

"Excellent. Excellent." He settles into the chair across from my desk, making himself comfortable in a way that suggests this isn't a quick check-in. "And you're finding everything... satisfactory? No obstacles? No complications?"

The way he says "complications" makes my pulse spike. "No complications. The cooperation from all departments has been excellent."

"Good. That's very good." He's watching me too closely, his expression pleasantly neutral in a way that feels dangerous. "And you're maintaining appropriate professional boundaries? I know it can be difficult when you're working so closely with leadership. Easy to let personal and professional lines blur."

My mouth goes dry. This isn't about the assessment. This is about Elliot.

"I'm maintaining complete independence," I say firmly. "My assessment is objective and thorough. There are no personal complications affecting my work."

"Of course not. I didn't mean to suggest otherwise." But his tone suggests exactly otherwise. "I'm just... making sure you understand how seriously the board takes the independence of this role. Your reputation is built on objectivity, isn't it? It would be unfortunate if anything called that into question."

He's not mentioning Elliot by name. Not referencing Saturday morning or the parking garage or anything specific. But the implication is crystal clear: he knows something, or suspects something, and he's warning me.

"My work speaks for itself," I say, lifting my chin even though my hands are shaking under the desk. "The board hired me specifically because of my reputation for independence and thoroughness. Nothing has changed that."

"I'm very glad to hear it." Harrison stands, smoothing his tie. "Well, I won't take up more of your time. I just wanted to touch base. Make sure everything is... appropriate."

After he leaves, I sit at my desk trying to control my breathing.

He knows. Or he's close enough to knowing that the distinction doesn't matter. Kevin must have mentioned seeing Elliot leave my apartment, or someone else saw something, or Harrison's just suspicious enough to start asking pointed questions.

Either way, this is real. This isn't paranoia or overthinking. Harrison Gordon is circling, looking for evidence that my relationship with Elliot is compromising my objectivity, waiting for the moment he can use it to destroy both our careers.

I close my eyes, willing myself to calm down.

This has to end. Not because I want it to—god, I don't want it to. But because I can't watch Harrison destroy Elliot's career. Can't watch everything Elliot's worked for dissolve because he's involved with his compliance officer. Can't risk my own reputation—twenty years of building credibility as an objective, independent assessor—being destroyed for a relationship that's temporary anyway.

Because it is temporary, isn't it?

I'm leaving in six weeks. I have fertility appointments scheduled for April. I have a plan for single motherhood that doesn't include space for a relationship with my CEO.

I've been lying to myself, pretending this could work somehow. That we could hide it long enough for my contract to end, then figure out the rest. That the feelings between us were enough to overcome the professional complications and the timeline mismatch and the fundamental incompatibility of our situations.

But Harrison's visit just shattered that illusion.

This isn't sustainable. This isn't safe. And continuing it is selfish—risking Elliot's position, risking my reputation, risking everything we've both worked for—for what? A few more weeks of stolen moments before I leave anyway?

The math doesn't work. The risk-reward calculation is entirely upside down.

I have to end this. For both our sakes.

The thought makes my chest ache so badly I have to press my hand against my sternum to make sure my heart is still beating.

I've never been happier than I've been these past weeks with Elliot. Never felt this connected to anyone, this seen and valued and wanted. Never imagined that at forty-one years old I could feel this way about someone—like I'm finally understanding what all those romantic comedies and love songs were talking about.

And I'm going to have to walk away from it.

Not today. I'm not strong enough to do it today. But soon. Before Harrison finds concrete evidence. Before this blows up and destroys us both.

THE WEEK PASSES in a strange kind of limbo. I avoid Elliot as much as possible at work—declining his lunch invitations, keeping our interactions brief and professional, making excuses when he texts asking to see me.

He knows something's wrong. I can see it in the way he watches me during the one meeting we both attend, in the concerned texts he sends that I respond to with brief, vague reassurances.

ELLIOT:

Are you okay? You've been distant.

ME:

I'm fine. Just busy with the assessment.

ELLIOT:

Can we talk? I feel like something's off.

ME:

Nothing's off. Just stressed about work. I'll
call you this weekend.

But I don't call him. Because talking to him means explaining what I've decided, and I'm not ready to say it out loud yet. Not ready to see the hurt in his eyes when I tell him we have to end this.

By Friday, I'm exhausted from the effort of avoiding him while maintaining professional appearances. I leave work early, claiming a headache—which isn't entirely a lie, since tension has been building behind my eyes all week.

At home, I pour a glass of wine and sit on my couch staring at my phone, knowing I should call Elliot, knowing I owe him an explanation for my distance this week.

But I'm not ready. Not yet.

I'm scrolling mindlessly through my phone when I see an email from Dr. Martinez's office. A reminder about my follow-up appointment in April—the one where we'll do the final consultation before scheduling the IUI procedure.

Does that plan still make sense? After Elliot, after feeling what a real relationship could be like, does going it alone still feel right?

I don't know. I don't know anything anymore except that I'm terrified and confused and so deeply in love with someone I'm going to have to leave.

My phone rings. Elliot.

I stare at it for a long moment before answering. "Hi."

"Hi." His voice is warm but concerned. "I've been worried about you. You've been avoiding me all week."

"I know. I'm sorry."

"Cassie, what's going on? Did something happen?"

I should tell him about Harrison's visit. Should explain that we're not safe, that this has to end before it destroys us both. Should be honest about the decision I've been circling all week.

But the words stick in my throat.

"I've just been thinking," I say instead. "About what we're doing. About the risks we're taking."

"The risks we've always been taking? Or did something specific happen?" His voice is careful, like he's trying to understand what shifted.

"Kevin from IT saw you leaving my apartment Saturday morning. And Harrison—" I stop, realizing I'm about to tell him. "Harrison came to my office Monday."

The silence on the other end is heavy. "What did he say?"

"That the board takes independence very seriously. That my reputation is built on objectivity and it would be unfortunate if anything called that into question." I take a shaky breath. "He didn't mention you by name. Didn't reference Saturday. But he didn't have to. The implication was clear."

"Son of a bitch." Elliot's voice is tight with anger. "He's fishing."

"Maybe. But he's also watching, Elliot. He's circling. And when he finds something—because he will find something eventually—he's going to use it to destroy both of us."

"Then we'll be more careful."

"How? You were at my apartment Saturday morning and someone saw you. We work in the same building. We're together constantly for legitimate work reasons, which makes it impossible to avoid each other, which means eventually someone's going to notice something." I press my hand to my forehead. "I can't do this. I can't watch you lose everything because of me."

"Cassie—"

"I need some time. To think. To figure out what I'm doing." It's not a complete lie, but it's not the whole truth either. "Can you give me that? Some space to think?"

The silence on the other end stretches so long I think he might have hung up. Then: "If that's what you need."

"It is. I'm sorry."

"Don't apologize. Just—" He pauses. "Just don't disappear on me, okay? When you're ready to talk, I'm here."

After we hang up, I sit in the darkness of my living room and let myself cry. For what I'm about to lose. For the relationship I'm going to have to end. For the happiness I've never felt before and probably won't feel again.

I've never been happier than I've been with Elliot. And that's exactly why I have to let him go.

THE WEEKEND PASSES in a blur of overthinking and wine and trying to convince myself I'm making the right decision.

By Monday, I've built enough walls around my heart that I can walk into Pierce and maintain professional distance. Can smile politely when I pass Elliot in the hallway. Can sit through a meeting with him and the executive team without my voice shaking.

Can pretend I'm not dying inside.

He sends a text Tuesday afternoon: *Can we talk?*

ME:

Not yet. I'm sorry.

Wednesday:

ELLIOT:

I miss you.

I don't respond to that one. Can't respond, because if I do, I'll fall apart.

By Thursday, he's stopped texting. And that hurts more than I expected—the silence, the absence, the growing distance I've created between us.

But it's necessary. It's the only way to protect him.

It's the only way to protect myself.

I throw myself into work, spending twelve-hour days at the office finishing the compliance assessment. The preliminary findings are coming together well—comprehensive, thorough, objective. No one will be able to question the quality of my work, even if they eventually learn about my relationship with Elliot.

Because the work is solid. Independent. Exactly what Pierce hired me to deliver.

It's the one thing I can control in a situation that feels increasingly out of control.

17

Elliot

"The Blaisdell team is getting nervous about the merger," Colton says as he settles on the chair across from my desk. "They need reassurance that we're committed and able. You need to be there."

I glance at my calendar, frowning. It's been four days since Cassie asked for space and I'd hoped we'd find time to talk in person. "How long?"

"A week, maybe two. Depends on how quickly we can resolve the operational concerns," he replies. "Joanna from legal will be with you, as well as Tom from operations, and I'm sending two of my analysts to handle the financial modeling."

Two weeks in San Diego with a team running intensive negotiations. Two weeks of being buried in merger details with Pierce's best people working the deal while Cassie's pulling away from me and I don't know how to stop it.

"We'll be there Monday morning," I tell Colton as relief floods his features.

"Good. You've worked hard on this, Elliot," he says. "We can't afford to lose it."

As he leaves my office, I tell myself maybe the distance will be good. Maybe Cassie needs space and I need perspective. Maybe when I get back, we can actually talk about whatever's going on instead of this painful dance of avoidance we've been doing since Harrison showed up at her office.

I text her before I leave for the airport:

> Heading to San Diego for Blaisdell negotiations. Probably gone a week or two. Can we talk when I get back?

Her response comes an hour later:

> Good luck with Blaisdell. We'll talk when you're back.

It's not exactly a yes. It's not a no. It's Cassie being careful, distant, giving nothing away.

I board the plane trying not to think about how much I miss her already.

SAN DIEGO CONSUMES ME COMPLETELY.

The team and I fall into a brutal rhythm—twelve-hour days of negotiations with Jennifer managing legal details, Tom coordinating operational integration plans, and Colton's analysts building financial models in real-time as terms evolve. Evenings are spent in conference rooms at the hotel, reviewing contracts and integration documentation, preparing for the next day's meetings. Early mornings are calls with Colton back in LA, keeping him updated on progress.

The Blaisdell executives are smart and cautious, questioning every detail of the compliance framework, pushing back on integration timelines, requiring constant reassurance that Pierce can actually deliver what we're promising.

I walk them through Cassie's compliance recommendations, explaining how her framework addresses each of their concerns. Jennifer backs me up with legal analysis. Tom shows them the operational roadmap. Together we make the case that this merger is achievable.

"Your compliance officer really knows her stuff," one of their VPs says during a break. "This framework is impressive."

"She's the best in the business," I say, and mean it.

Everything about this deal has Cassie's fingerprints on it. Her thoroughness. Her strategic thinking. Her ability to see around corners and anticipate problems before they surface. Without her assessment, this merger would be a disaster. With it, it's actually achievable.

I should call her. Tell her how critical her work has been. Tell her that she's making this possible.

But every time I pull out my phone, I remember the distance in her voice the last time we talked. The walls she's building between us. The space she asked for that feels less like breathing room and more like preparation for goodbye.

So I don't call.

I just throw myself deeper into the work.

By the end of the second week, we've reached tentative agreement on all major terms. The Blaisdell merger is happening—pending final board approval from both companies, but the hard work is done. Integration will take months, but the framework is solid.

Cassie's framework. Her compliance recommendations that made this possible.

I should feel victorious. This is a major win for Pierce, a validation of my leadership, concrete evidence that I can handle complex deals and deliver results.

Instead, I just feel tired and empty and desperate to get back to LA to see Cassie.

We fly back on a Friday evening, landing at LAX around seven PM. The executive floor will be empty by now—everyone gone for the weekend—but I head to the office anyway. Need to catch up on emails, review what I missed during two weeks in San Diego, prepare for Monday's return to normal operations.

The building is quiet when I arrive, just security and a few scattered lights from people working late. I take the elevator to the executive floor, and the silence feels heavier than usual. Two weeks away and the office feels unfamiliar, like I'm walking through a space that used to be mine but isn't quite anymore.

I'm heading toward my office when I pass Cassie's door.

And stop.

Someone else is sitting at her desk. A man I don't recognize, probably late fifties, reviewing documents on a laptop. He looks up when I pause in the doorway, gives a polite nod.

"Can I help you?" he asks.

"I'm—" I stop, disoriented. "Where's Cassie Reynolds?"

"Ms. Reynolds left the company a week ago. Family emergency. I'm Ronald Bryson, brought in temporarily to coordinate final assessment details with her remotely." He stands, extending a hand. "You must be Mr. Walker. Good to meet you."

I shake his hand automatically, but my brain is stuck on his words.

A week ago. While I was in San Diego.

"She left?" My voice sounds strange to my own ears. "When exactly?"

"I started Thursday, so I believe her last day was that Monday or Tuesday." Ronald looks at me with concern. "I assumed you were aware—HR sent notification to all executives."

I mumble something polite before walking to my office on autopilot. Pull up my email, scroll back two weeks, searching through the flood of Blaisdell messages and merger documentation and integration plans.

There. Buried in the middle of day three of San Diego negotiations, when I was drowning in contracts and barely looking at anything not directly related to the merger.

Subject: Staff Change Notification - Cassandra Reynolds

Effective immediately, Cassandra Reynolds has requested early termination of her contract due to family emergency. Ms. Reynolds' mother suffered a fall resulting in a broken hip and requires care during recovery. The board has approved Ms. Reynolds' request. She will complete her preliminary assessment findings remotely from Portland, Oregon.

Ronald Bryson (external consultant) will coordinate with Ms. Reynolds and finalize assessment details on-site.

I look at the date and time.

It had been sent while I was in a meeting with the Blaisdell executive team. By the time it made it into my inbox, it was buried under dozens of other messages. I must have scanned it, noted it, filed it away as something to deal with later because Blaisdell was consuming every available brain cell.

She left. A few days ago. And I didn't even notice.

I sit at my desk staring at the email, trying to process. Her mother broke her hip. She had to leave to care for her. That's a legitimate emergency, a real reason to end her contract early.

But the timing. Asking for space and then submitting her termination request a week later.

This wasn't just about her mother.

I pull out my phone and call her. It rings four times, then goes to voicemail.

"Cassie, it's me. I just got back from San Diego and found out you left. I—" I stop, not knowing what to say. "Call me. Please. I need to talk to you."

I hang up and immediately text: *Just found out you're gone. Why didn't you tell me? Call me.*

The text shows delivered but not read.

I try calling again. Voicemail again.

My chest is tight, breathing difficult. She left. She asked for space, I gave it to her by being buried in San Diego for two weeks, and she used that time to leave without saying goodbye.

No. That's not fair, Walker.

Her mother broke her hip. That's not something you plan or use as an excuse. That's a real emergency that required a real response.

But she could have told me. Could have called or texted or sent some kind of message beyond a formal HR notification I didn't even see for three days.

Unless she wanted to leave without having to face me. Without having to explain or justify or deal with me trying to convince her to stay.

I lean back in my chair, staring at my office ceiling, trying to figure out what I'm supposed to do with this information.

Cassie's gone.

She's in Portland taking care of her mother. The assessment will be completed remotely. And I'm here, a week behind on understanding what happened, with no idea how to fix something I didn't even know was broken until it was already over.

THE WEEKEND PASSES in a blur of trying and failing to reach Cassie.

Saturday morning:

> Please call me. I need to know you're okay.

Saturday afternoon:

> I'm worried about you. About your mother. Just let me know you're alright.

Saturday evening:

> Cassie, please.

Sunday morning she finally responds:

CASSIE:

> My mother is recovering. I'm fine. I'll have the preliminary findings to you by end of month.

Professional. Distant. Like I'm just another executive waiting for her assessment instead of someone who's been sleeping in her bed, learning her body, falling for her despite every rational reason not to.

That's not what I'm asking about, I text back. *Can we talk? Really talk?*

Her response takes an hour:

CASSIE:

> There's nothing to talk about. I'm here with my mother. You're there running Pierce. That's how it should be.

ME:

> That's not how it should be and you know it.

No response to that one.

Sunday evening I try calling again. She answers this time, and the sound of her voice makes my chest ache.

"Elliot."

"Hey. I've been trying to reach you all weekend."

"I know. I'm sorry. I've been busy with my mom. Getting her settled, coordinating with physical therapists, making sure she has everything she needs." She sounds tired. Stressed. But also guarded, like she's reading from a script.

"How is she?"

"She'll be fine. The surgery went well. Recovery is going to take six to eight weeks, but the prognosis is good."

"That's good. That's really good." I'm pacing my bedroom now, phone pressed to my ear. "Cassie, why didn't you tell me you were leaving? I had to find out from HR. From some guy sitting in your office."

"I didn't plan it. My mom fell, she needed help, I had to go," she says. "Everything happened very quickly."

"You could have called. Texted. Something."

"You were in San Diego dealing with Blaisdell," she says. "I didn't want to distract you from something important."

"You're important. More important than any merger."

Silence on the other end. Then: "Elliot, we both knew this was temporary. My contract was ending in four weeks anyway. This just moved up the timeline."

"This isn't about the timeline and you know it," I say. "This is about you running away."

"I'm not running away. I'm taking care of my mother."

"And avoiding me. Avoiding us," I say. "Avoiding the conversation we need to have about whatever's been going on since Harrison showed up at your office."

More silence. When she speaks again, her voice is quieter. "What conversation do you want to have, Elliot? The one where we acknowledge that we risked both our careers for something that was never going to work anyway?"

The words hit like a punch. "That's not what this was."

"Wasn't it? I was always leaving in six months. I have plans that don't include sneaking around with my CEO and hoping Harrison doesn't destroy us both." She takes a breath. "I'm protecting my career, Elliot. Twenty years of building a reputation for independence and objectivity. I can't throw that away."

"So that's it? You're just done? You're choosing your career over what we have?"

"What we had. Past tense." Her voice is firm now, resolved. "I care about you. But I care about my professional reputation more. And I'm not willing to risk it anymore."

The words should make me angry. Should make me defensive or hurt or ready to fight.

Instead, they just make me tired. Because I hear what she's really saying: this is over, and she's not changing her mind.

"Okay," I say quietly. "If that's what you want."

"It is."

"Then I hope your mom recovers quickly. And I hope—" I stop, trying to find words that don't hurt to say. "I hope you find whatever it is you're looking for."

I hang up before she can respond.

Stand in my bedroom staring at my phone, waiting for her to call back. Waiting for her to say she didn't mean it, that she's scared and protecting herself but she doesn't actually want this to be over.

She doesn't call.

And I'm left standing in the house where we spent Christmas together, where we gardened and cooked and pretended we could make this work, feeling more alone than I've ever felt in my life.

WORK BECOMES MY ESCAPE.

The Blaisdell merger moves into final implementation phase, which means endless meetings about integration timelines and operational coordination and change management strategies. I throw myself into it completely—fourteen-hour days, weekends in the office, constant calls with department heads and project managers.

Colton notices. "You're going to burn out if you keep this pace."

"I'm fine. Just want to make sure integration goes smoothly."

"You've been working eighty-hour weeks since you got back from San Diego," he says, concern evident on his face. "That's not sustainable."

"I'm handling it."

He gives me a look that says he doesn't believe me but he's not going to push. "Just don't kill yourself over this merger, okay? It's important, but it's not worth destroying your health."

If he only knew. I'm not working like this because of the merger. I'm working like this because if I stop, if I slow down, I'll have to think about Cassie. About the fact that she chose her career over us. About the fact that I let her walk away without really fighting for her.

About the fact that I might be in love with someone who didn't love me back enough to take a risk.

Declan shows up at my office one evening in late February, finds me still at my desk at eight PM reviewing integration documentation.

"Walk. We need to talk."

"I'm busy."

"You're always busy lately. That's the problem." He closes my office door and sits down uninvited. "What's going on? And don't say nothing, because I know you better than that."

"Nothing's going on. I'm just focused on work."

"You're burying yourself in work. There's a difference." He's watching me with that analytical expression that misses nothing. "This is about Cassie, isn't it? She left."

"For a family emergency. Her mother broke her hip."

"And you haven't talked to her since."

"She made it clear she didn't want to talk. She chose her

career over what we had. Said her professional reputation was more important than our relationship." The words still sting saying them out loud. "So I'm respecting that choice and moving on."

"Are you? Because from where I'm sitting, you look like someone who's barely holding it together."

"I'm fine."

"You're working eighty hours a week and avoiding everyone who cares about you. That's not fine." Declan leans forward. "Look, I don't know exactly what happened between you and Cassie. But I know what I saw at Christmas—two people who were really happy together. And I know what I see now—you being miserable and pretending you're not."

"She left, Declan," I say, exhaling. "She chose her career over us. What am I supposed to do about that?"

"Did she though? Choose her career over you?" He's watching me carefully. "Or did she choose to protect you by removing herself from a situation that was putting both of you at risk?"

"She literally said her professional reputation was more important than our relationship."

"And you believed her?"

The question stops me. "Why wouldn't I?"

"Because she spent Christmas at your house. She met your family. She let herself care about you enough to risk everything she'd worked for." Declan leans back. "That's not someone who puts career over everything. That's someone who got scared and ran."

"Even if that's true, it doesn't change anything. She's gone," I say. "She made her choice."

"So make yours. Decide whether you're going to accept that choice or fight for what you want."

After Declan leaves, I sit in my office staring at nothing, his words circling in my head.

Did Cassie leave to protect herself? Or to protect me?

She said it was about her career, her reputation, her professional credibility. But what if that was just easier than admitting she was scared? Easier than acknowledging that she cared enough to sacrifice what we had to keep me safe from Harrison's scrutiny?

I don't know. And I can't know without talking to her, which she's made clear she doesn't want to do.

So I go back to work. Back to the merger integration and the endless meetings and the exhausting pace that keeps me too busy to think.

18

—

Cassie

Portland in late February is exactly as miserable as I feel—gray skies, constant drizzle, temperatures hovering just above freezing. The kind of weather that seeps into your bones and makes everything feel heavy and hopeless.

Perfect match for my mood.

I've been here two weeks, living in my mother's apartment at Cascade Falls Senior Living, a 55+ community that's nicer than most—well-maintained grounds, activities center, on-site medical staff. Her apartment is a spacious two-bedroom unit with updated kitchen and a view of the courtyard garden, which would be lovely if the sun ever came out.

My mother is recovering well from her hip surgery. The pin they inserted is holding, physical therapy is progressing on schedule, and the pain is manageable with medication. She's frustrated with the limitations—hates using the walker, complains about not being able to drive, gets annoyed when I hover too much trying to help.

"I'm not an invalid, Cassandra," she says for the

hundredth time when I try to help her from the chair to the walker. "I can get up on my own."

"I know. I'm just—"

"Hovering. You're hovering." But she lets me steady her anyway, and once she's stable on the walker, she pats my hand. "I appreciate you being here, honey. I do. But you don't need to treat me like I'm made of glass."

"Sorry." I step back, giving her space to navigate to the bathroom on her own.

She's right that I am hovering. But it's easier to focus on her recovery than to think about anything else. Easier to obsess over her medication schedule and physical therapy exercises than to acknowledge the hollow ache in my chest that hasn't eased since I left Los Angeles.

Since I left Elliot.

I've been trying not to think about him. Trying to focus on the practical tasks in front of me—helping my mother, finishing the compliance assessment remotely, coordinating with Ronald Bryson who's handling the on-site details at Pierce. Trying to convince myself I made the right choice by leaving.

It's not working.

I miss him constantly. Miss his voice, his laugh, the way he looked at me like I was the most important person in his world. Miss the quiet mornings in his kitchen, the conversations on his patio, the feeling of falling asleep in his arms knowing I was exactly where I belonged.

I've been crying at random times—in the grocery store when I see his favorite coffee, in my mother's kitchen when I'm making eggs the way he taught me, late at night when I can't sleep and the apartment is too quiet. I try to hide it, but my mother notices everything.

"You've been here two weeks and you've cried more than I've seen you cry in your entire adult life," she says one evening. We're sitting in her living room—her in the recliner with her leg elevated, me curled up on the couch pretending to read a book I haven't absorbed a single word of.

"I'm just tired. And worried about you."

"Liar." She's watching me with that maternal X-ray vision that sees through every deflection. "This isn't about me. This is about whatever—or whoever—you left behind in Los Angeles."

I don't respond, just stare at my book.

"Cassie." Her voice is gentler now. "Talk to me. What's going on?"

"Nothing. I'm fine."

"You're not fine. You're miserable. You barely eat, you cry constantly, and you're distracted all the time. I asked you to pass me the remote three times yesterday before you heard me."

"I'm just stressed about work." It's not entirely a lie. The assessment is consuming hours of my day, coordinating remotely with Ronald, reviewing his on-site findings, finalizing my recommendations. "And adjusting to Portland. And worrying about you."

"And pining for someone you left behind."

The accuracy of that statement makes my throat tight. "Mom—"

"I'm not blind, honey. Or stupid. You came here because I needed help, yes. But you also came here running from something. Or someone." She shifts in her chair, wincing slightly at the movement. "Want to tell me about it?"

I set down the book I'm not reading and pull my knees

up to my chest. "There was someone. In LA. Someone I was seeing."

"And?"

"And it was complicated. He's—" I stop, trying to figure out how to explain without explaining too much. "He's in a position where our relationship could cause professional problems for both of us. So I ended it. To protect both our careers."

"Did he want you to end it?"

"No," I reply, "But it was the right thing to do."

"For him or for you?"

"For both of us." I wrap my arms tighter around my knees. "It was never going to work long-term anyway. I had plans—have plans—that don't include a relationship right now."

"The fertility treatments."

"Yes. The treatments are scheduled. That's what I should be focusing on—not some relationship that was temporary anyway."

My mother is quiet for a long moment. "Your father and I —we had our problems. Obviously. He left when you were eight, and that was devastating for both of us. But before that, before things fell apart, we were happy. Really happy." She's looking at her hands now, at her wedding ring she still wears despite thirty-two years of divorce. "I don't regret those years with him, even knowing how it ended. Because feeling that kind of connection with someone—being truly happy with another person—that's rare. And precious. And worth the risk of getting hurt."

"Mom—"

"I know you're scared. I know your engagement to Brad ended badly and you're trying to protect yourself by controlling everything—your career, your timeline, your plan for motherhood," she says. "But life doesn't work that way, honey. You can't plan away the risk of being hurt. You can only decide whether the person is worth the risk."

"It's not just about being hurt," I say. "It's about professional reputation. About jeopardizing everything I've worked for."

"Is it? Or is that just easier than admitting you're in love with him?"

I stare at her.

Of course she's right.

I am in love with Elliot. Have been for weeks, maybe months. And I'm terrified of what that means, how vulnerable it makes me, how much I could lose if I let myself fully admit it.

"It doesn't matter if I love him," I say quietly. "The circumstances make it impossible. And I'm not willing to risk both our careers for something that might not even last."

"So you're going to spend the rest of your life wondering 'what if' instead of fighting for what you want?"

"I'm being realistic."

"You're being a coward."

The blunt assessment stings. "That's not fair."

"Isn't it? You ran, Cassie. You used my accident as an excuse to leave before you had to face your feelings or make a real choice about what you wanted." Her voice softens. "I love you, and I'm grateful you're here helping me. But we both know I would have been fine with the facility staff and my friends. You didn't have to leave your job two weeks early. You chose to because it gave you an out."

I can't argue with that because it's true. My mother

would have been fine. The staff here is excellent, her friends are supportive, and her recovery is progressing well. I came to Portland because she needed help, yes. But I also came because I needed an escape from the impossible situation I'd created with Elliot.

"I don't know how to fix it," I admit. "Even if I wanted to —and I'm not saying I do—I don't know how to make it work. The professional complications are real. Harrison Gordon was already circling. If we'd stayed together, it would have destroyed both our careers eventually."

"So you destroyed the relationship instead to save the careers?"

"Yes."

"And how's that working out for you?"

I don't answer because the answer is obvious. I'm miserable. My career is intact but I've never been more unhappy in my life.

My mother sighs. "Look, honey, I can't tell you what to do. But I can tell you that thirty-two years after your father left, I still wish I'd fought harder to save our marriage. I let pride and hurt and fear of looking foolish keep me from really trying. And I've regretted it every day since."

"You and Dad were married with a child," I say. "Elliot and I were together for a few months."

"Time doesn't matter. Feeling matters. And from where I'm sitting, you feel more for this man after a few months than you ever felt for Brad after ten years."

She's right about that too. What I feel for Elliot is so much deeper, more consuming, more real than anything I felt during my decade with Brad. With Brad, I was comfortable but never truly happy. With Elliot, I was terrified and vulnerable and more alive than I've ever been.

"I need to think," I say, standing up. "Do you need anything before I go to bed?"

"Just for you to stop lying to yourself about what you want."

I escape to the guest bedroom and close the door, then sit on the bed staring at my phone.

Three missed calls from Elliot over the past two weeks. A dozen texts I've barely responded to. The last one, from four days ago:

ELLIOT:

> I know you don't want to talk. But I hope you know I'm here if you change your mind.

I should delete them. Should block his number and move on with my life. Should focus on my April appointment and the fertility treatments and the plan I had before Elliot complicated everything.

Instead, I scroll through our text history, reading old messages from when we were happy. When we were sneaking around and stealing moments and pretending we could make it work.

Missing you he'd texted one night in January.

Me too I'd responded.

Simple exchanges that now feel like they're from a different lifetime. When we were both still pretending this could work. When I hadn't yet realized how impossible it all was.

I set down my phone and lie back on the bed, staring at the ceiling.

My mother thinks I'm being a coward. Maybe she's right. Maybe I ran instead of fighting for what I wanted. Maybe I used professional complications as an excuse to protect myself from the terrifying vulnerability of being in love.

But even if that's true, I don't know how to fix it now. Don't know how to walk back my decision to leave, my cold phone conversation with Elliot where I told him my career mattered more than us, my weeks of radio silence that clearly communicated I wanted nothing to do with him.

I don't know how to undo the damage I've done.

But first, I have an assessment to complete, one I need to send to Ronald Bryson, my replacement.

I'm just finalizing recommendations and doing a last review before submitting to the board. It's good work, comprehensive and thorough and completely objective despite my personal feelings for Elliot.

I made sure of that. Made sure that every finding is defensible, every recommendation is evidence-based, every assessment of his leadership is fair and accurate. If anyone ever questions my objectivity, the work itself will be the proof that I maintained professional standards regardless of my personal involvement.

It's the one thing I can control. The one thing I can be proud of in this entire mess.

FRIDAY MORNING, I wake up feeling off.

Not sick exactly, just... wrong. My stomach is unsettled, my head feels foggy, and there's a general sense of unease I can't quite pin down.

"You okay?" my mother asks when I emerge from the bedroom looking pale. "You don't look well."

"I'm fine. Just didn't sleep great."

"You should eat something. You've barely been eating all week."

She's right about that. Food hasn't been appealing lately—everything tastes bland or makes my stomach turn. I've lost weight since coming to Portland, my clothes hanging looser than they should.

I force down some toast and tea, then escape to my laptop to send off the final compliance assessment to Ronald.

By midday, the nausea is worse. I'm lightheaded and tired and seriously considering whether I'm coming down with something.

"You look terrible," my mother announces when she finds me in the bathroom, splashing cold water on my face. "Are you getting sick?"

"Maybe. I don't know." I dry my face, studying my reflection. Dark circles under my eyes. Pale skin. Exhausted expression. "I feel weird."

"Weird how?"

"Nauseous. Tired. Just off." I press my hand to my stomach. "Maybe I ate something bad."

"Or maybe you're pregnant."

The words hang in the air between us.

I turn to stare at my mother. "What did you say?"

"Pregnant. You're exhausted, emotional, nauseous, not eating." She's watching me with concern now. "When was your last period?"

My mind goes blank. *When was my last period?*

I've been so consumed with work and Elliot and the decision to leave LA that I haven't been tracking. Haven't thought about it. Haven't noticed—

Oh god.

"Cassie?" My mother's voice is sharp now. "When was your last period?"

"I don't—" I'm mentally counting back, trying to remember. December. It must have been December because we spent Christmas together and I definitely wasn't having my period then. Which means—

"I need to sit down," I manage, my knees suddenly weak.

My mother helps me to the couch, hovering with the same concern I've been showing her for two weeks.

"You didn't know?" she asks gently.

"I've been stressed. I wasn't tracking. I didn't—" I press my hands to my face. "Oh god. We were careful. We used condoms every time. How could—"

"Condoms fail, honey," she says. "It happens."

I'm doing math in my head. Christmas week. That's when it must have happened. We were together multiple times, careful each time, but condoms aren't foolproof. One must have failed. One microscopic failure and now—

"I need a pregnancy test," I say, standing up too quickly and having to grab the arm of the couch for balance. "I need to know for sure before I panic."

"There's a drugstore two blocks away. I'll stay here. You go."

I grab my coat and keys and walk to the drugstore in a daze. The clerk at the counter gives me a knowing look when I buy three different pregnancy tests—different brands, different sensitivities, as if multiple tests will somehow change the result.

Back at my mother's apartment, I lock myself in the bathroom with all three tests.

My hands are shaking as I open the first package. Read the instructions twice to make sure I understand even though they're straightforward. Follow them exactly, then set the test on the counter and force myself to wait the required three minutes.

The longest three minutes of my life.

When I finally look at the test, there are two very clear pink lines.

Pregnant.

I take the second test. Two lines.

The third test. A plus sign.

All three tests, three different brands, all saying the same thing.

I'm pregnant with Elliot's baby.

19

Elliot

THE BOARD MEETING is scheduled for Monday morning.

I've known it was coming—the preliminary compliance assessment findings were due end of February, and the board always reviews major assessments in full session. But knowing it's coming doesn't make me any less anxious about it.

Especially because Harrison Gordon has been circling all week.

"He's been asking questions," Colton tells me Friday afternoon. "Casual questions about the assessment timeline, about whether we've seen preliminary findings yet, about Cassie's departure."

"What kind of questions?"

"The kind that suggest he's looking for something." Colton leans against my office doorframe. "I don't know what he knows or thinks he knows, but he's definitely hunting for ammunition."

Great. So Harrison's planning something for Monday's board meeting. Probably going to try to use Cassie's early departure against me somehow, suggest her assessment is incomplete or compromised or that my judgment is questionable for letting the compliance officer leave early.

I've been dreading this meeting for a week, running through scenarios in my head. None of them end well.

"The assessment is solid," I tell Colton, trying to convince myself as much as him. "Cassie's work is always thorough. Whatever Harrison's planning, he won't be able to undermine the actual findings."

"I hope you're right."

So do I.

Monday morning arrives too quickly.

The boardroom is full when I arrive ten minutes early—all twelve board members, Colton, Joanna, and Ronald Bryson, the consultant who's been coordinating final assessment details with Cassie remotely.

Harrison is already seated, looking pleased with himself in a way that makes my stomach tight.

Melinda calls the meeting to order promptly at nine AM.

"First order of business is the preliminary compliance assessment findings," Melinda announces. "Mr. Bryson, you've been coordinating with Ms. Reynolds. Can you walk us through the key findings?"

Ronald stands, pulling up a presentation on the screen. "Of course. Ms. Reynolds completed a comprehensive operational and leadership assessment over a twelve-week period from October through February. Her findings are detailed in the full report you all received Friday, but I'll summarize the key points."

He clicks to the first slide. A bullet-point summary of assessment scope and methodology.

"The assessment covered all major operational areas—risk management, compliance protocols, interdepartmental coordination, leadership effectiveness, and corporate governance standards. Ms. Reynolds conducted over fifty interviews with staff across all levels, reviewed five years of operational documentation, and analyzed decision-making processes for major strategic initiatives."

Next slide. Key findings.

As he begins to summarize Cassie's findings, I'm watching Harrison, waiting for him to pounce. But he's just sitting there with that pleased expression, like he's waiting for something.

Ronald continues. "The assessment identifies CEO Elliot Walker's leadership as a key strength. Strategic decision-making is well-documented and transparent. Executive team coordination is effective. The response to compliance gaps identified during the assessment period was prompt and appropriate."

"I have a question." Harrison's voice cuts through Ronald's presentation.

Here it comes.

"Of course, Mr. Gordon," Melinda says.

Harrison leans forward, his expression pleasant but his tone pointed. "I'm sure Ms. Reynolds' work is thorough. But I have concerns about the objectivity of this assessment given certain... irregularities."

"What irregularities?" Melinda asks.

"Ms. Reynolds left her contract two weeks early, citing a family emergency. Which may be legitimate—I'm not questioning that. But it does raise questions about whether she completed a thorough assessment or rushed through findings to accommodate her personal timeline."

It's a careful attack. Not directly accusing Cassie of anything concrete, just raising doubts.

"The assessment is quite comprehensive," Ronald says. "Sixty-eight pages of detailed analysis with extensive supporting documentation—"

"I'm sure it's lengthy," Harrison interrupts. "But length doesn't equal objectivity. Especially when there may have been personal factors affecting Ms. Reynolds' judgment."

"What personal factors?" Melinda's voice has an edge now.

Harrison looks directly at me. "Mr. Walker and Ms. Reynolds knew each other prior to this engagement, didn't they? From Stanford?"

"Yes," I say carefully. "Cassie was my mentor in a business leadership program seven years ago. We hadn't seen each other since then until she was hired for this assessment."

"And once she was hired, you spent considerable time together outside of work contexts, didn't you?" Harrison's watching me closely. "I've heard from multiple sources that the two of you had extensive personal interaction during the assessment period."

My chest tightens. He's fishing, looking for me to confirm something he suspects but can't prove.

"We worked closely together for twelve weeks," I say evenly. "Some interaction outside strict office hours is inevitable in an intensive assessment."

"I'm talking about personal interaction. Social occasions," Harrison says. "Time spent together that had nothing to do with the assessment."

"Harrison, what exactly are you implying?" Melinda's voice is sharp.

"I'm implying that there may have been a personal relationship between Mr. Walker and Ms. Reynolds that compromised her objectivity. A relationship that went beyond professional courtesy or prior acquaintance."

The room is very quiet now.

"Do you have evidence of this alleged relationship?" Melinda asks.

Harrison hesitates—just for a second, but it's enough to tell me he doesn't have anything concrete. "I have reports from multiple sources about them being seen together—"

"Seen together doing what, exactly?" Patricia asks. "Having work meetings? Lunch discussions about the assessment? Or something actually inappropriate?"

"I... the nature of their interactions suggested more than professional collaboration," Harrison replies.

"Suggested to whom? And based on what specific evidence?" Melinda's tone is getting colder. "Harrison, if you're going to make accusations about impropriety, you need to be specific. Not vague insinuations based on unidentified sources."

Harrison's expression tightens. "I'm raising legitimate concerns about objectivity—"

"Based on speculation," Melinda interrupts. "Ms. Reynolds is no longer employed by Pierce. Her contract ended two weeks ago. Whatever personal relationship she may or may not have with Mr. Walker—whether as former student, colleague, friend, or anything else—is no longer relevant to this board's business."

"It's relevant if it compromised the assessment—"

"Did it?" Melinda looks at Ronald. "You've reviewed Ms. Reynolds' work extensively. Do you see any evidence of bias or compromised objectivity?"

"No," Ronald says firmly. "Ms. Reynolds' methodology is sound. Every conclusion is supported by documented evidence—interview notes, operational data, decision-making records. Her analysis is thorough and appropriately critical."

"Appropriately critical?" Harrison seizes on this. "So she was critical of Mr. Walker's leadership?"

"She identified areas for improvement, yes. Succession planning, interdepartmental communication protocols, compliance documentation standardization." Ronald pulls up another slide. "Ms. Reynolds identified seventeen operational issues across all departments and made specific recommendations for each. This isn't a whitewash job. It's a legitimate, thorough assessment that includes both strengths and areas needing work."

"Which could all be strategically designed to appear objective while actually protecting—"

"Harrison." Melinda's voice cuts through his speculation. "Unless you have concrete evidence that specific findings in this assessment are inaccurate or unsupported by data, this is pure speculation. And frankly, it's starting to sound like a personal vendetta rather than legitimate oversight."

Harrison's face flushes. "I'm trying to protect this board from accepting a potentially compromised assessment—"

"The assessment stands on its own merits," Patricia says. "I've read it twice. It's comprehensive, well-documented, and includes plenty of critical findings. If Ms. Reynolds was trying to make Elliot look good regardless of reality, she did a poor job of it because there are substantial recommendations for improvement throughout."

Several other board members nod agreement.

"Furthermore," Melinda adds, "Ms. Reynolds' professional reputation is built on independence and objectivity. She's conducted assessments for dozens of companies over twenty years. The idea that she would suddenly compromise her professional standards—the foundation of her entire career—strains credibility without concrete evidence."

Harrison sputters. "So we're just going to ignore the possibility—"

"We're going to evaluate the work product we hired her to deliver," Melinda says firmly. "Which appears to be thorough, objective, and exactly what we contracted for. Whatever personal relationship may or may not exist between Ms. Reynolds and Mr. Walker is irrelevant now that her employment has ended."

She looks around the table. "Does anyone have concerns about specific findings in this assessment? Actual substantive questions about the work itself?"

Silence.

"Then I move that we accept Ms. Reynolds' preliminary assessment findings and direct management to begin implementing her recommendations. All in favor?"

Ten hands go up. Only Harrison and one other board member abstain.

"Motion carries." Melinda makes a note. "The assessment is accepted. We'll expect quarterly progress reports on implementation of Ms. Reynolds' recommendations."

Harrison is staring at the table, his jaw tight. His attempt to undermine the assessment failed completely. He raised vague concerns about personal relationships and objectivity, but without concrete evidence, the board shut him down and evaluated the work on its merits.

And Cassie's work is so thorough, so well-documented, so appropriately critical that even Harrison's insinuations couldn't touch it.

The meeting continues with other business, but I'm barely listening.

Cassie protected both of us. She knew questions might come up about our relationship—whether Harrison had evidence or not, she knew it was possible. So she made sure her work was so rigorous, so objective, so thoroughly documented that it wouldn't matter. Even when Harrison raised doubts, the assessment stood on its own merits.

She didn't just protect me by leaving. She protected me by being so good at her job that no one could question it.

After the meeting ends, I head back to my office. I sit at my desk and pull up the assessment again, reading through sections I've already memorized. Every recommendation is supported by evidence. Every criticism is fair and constructive. Every strength is documented with specific examples.

This is someone who cared more about protecting my career than her own comfort.

This is someone who just might love me, even if she was too scared to say it.

And I let her go thinking I believed she chose her career over us.

But her contract is over. She's no longer Pierce's compliance officer. The professional complications that made her leave—they don't exist anymore. Harrison tried to use our relationship against us and failed. The assessment is accepted, her work validated.

There's nothing stopping us now except the fear that made her run.

I pull out my phone and start searching for flights to Portland.

20

———

Cassie

I'VE BEEN WALKING for over an hour, circling the grounds of Cascade Falls Senior Living like the answers to my impossible situation might appear if I just keep moving.

They don't.

Three days since I took those pregnancy tests. Three days of trying to figure out what I'm supposed to do with this information.

I'm pregnant with Elliot's baby. The man I love, the man I left to protect, the man who probably thinks I chose my career over him—he's going to be a father and he doesn't even know it.

I have to tell him. I know I have to tell him. But every time I pick up my phone to call, I freeze.

What am I supposed to say? *Hey, remember when I told you my career was more important than us? Well, surprise—I'm pregnant and everything I said was a lie because I was actually trying to protect you from Harrison but now there's a baby so all that sacrifice was pointless anyway.*

God, what a mess.

The Portland morning is gray and damp, typical for early March. I pull my jacket tighter as I walk past the community gardens, the activity center, the covered seating areas where residents gather when the weather's better than this.

My mother is doing well. Really well. She's graduated from walker to cane, regained most of her mobility, is increasingly independent. The physical therapist says she'll be back to full function within another few weeks.

Which means my excuse for being here is rapidly disappearing.

I need to figure out what comes next. Where I'm going to live—San Francisco with Lauren? Back to LA? Stay in Portland near my mother? And when am I going to tell Elliot about the baby?

My hand drifts to my stomach, still flat, showing no sign of the life growing inside. Eight weeks pregnant. By the time I have the baby, it'll be October. Fall. Everything in my life is about to change and I have no idea how to prepare for it.

I wanted a baby. Planned for one. Made appointments and selected donors and constructed a timeline for single motherhood.

But not like this. Not accidentally. Not with Elliot. Not when everything is so impossibly complicated.

Except—is it really that complicated anymore?

My contract with Pierce is over. The assessment is submitted. I'm no longer employed by the company, no longer in a position where my relationship with Elliot creates a conflict of interest.

The professional complications that made me leave— they're gone now, aren't they?

Unless Harrison finds out somehow. Unless the board questions my objectivity after the fact. Unless my entire career gets destroyed because I got pregnant by the CEO I was supposed to be monitoring.

My phone buzzes in my pocket. My mother.

MOM:

Where are you? Come back to the apartment.

ME:

Still walking. Need more time to think.

MOM:

Come back now. You have a visitor.

I stop walking, my heart suddenly racing.
A visitor? Here? In Portland?

ME:

Who?

MOM:

Just come home. Building C, remember? Don't make him wait too long.

Him.
Oh god.
Elliot.
Elliot is here. At my mother's apartment. Right now.

My hands are shaking as I stare at my phone, trying to process this information.

He came. He flew to Portland. He's at my mother's apartment waiting for me.

Why? Why would he come here after three weeks of silence? After I told him my career was more important? After I made it clear I was choosing to walk away?

Unless—unless he knows. Unless somehow he figured out I'm pregnant and he's here to—what? Confront me? Demand answers?

No. That doesn't make sense. How would he know? I haven't told anyone except my mother.

I force myself to breathe. To think.

Maybe this isn't about the pregnancy. Maybe he's here for some other reason. Maybe there's a problem with the assessment, or Harrison raised questions, or the board needs clarification on something.

Or maybe—and this thought makes my chest tight with hope and terror—maybe he's here because he figured out why I really left.

I start walking back toward Building C, my pace quickening with each step. By the time I reach my mother's building, I'm nearly running, my heart pounding so hard I can feel it in my throat.

I take the stairs to the second floor, not trusting myself to wait for the elevator. Stop outside apartment 217, trying to catch my breath and settle my nerves.

Elliot is on the other side of this door.

The man I love. The father of my baby. The person I've been trying not to think about for three weeks because thinking about him hurts too much.

I'm not ready for this. I don't know what I'm going to say. I haven't figured out how to tell him about the pregnancy or explain why I left or—

The door opens.

My mother is standing there with her cane, giving me a look that's equal parts sympathy and exasperation.

"About time," she says quietly. "He's been waiting twenty minutes. Don't leave him hanging much longer—he looks like he's about to jump out of his skin."

"Mom, I don't—I can't—"

"Yes, you can. And you will." She squeezes my arm as she passes me. "I'm going to visit Dorothy in 315 for a while. You two need privacy."

Then she's gone, leaving me standing in the doorway.

I step inside and close the door behind me.

Elliot is standing in the middle of the living room, looking completely out of place in his dark jeans and button-down shirt, his hair slightly messed like he's been running his hands through it. When he sees me, his whole face changes—relief and longing and something that looks like barely controlled emotion.

"Cassie."

Just my name, but the way he says it makes my eyes burn with tears I'm trying not to cry.

"Elliot." My voice comes out steadier than I expected. "What are you doing here?"

"I came to tell you what happened at the board meeting yesterday."

My stomach drops. "The assessment?"

"Harrison tried to undermine it. Claimed there might have been a personal relationship between us that compromised your objectivity."

Oh god. "What did the board say?"

"They shut him down. He had no proof of anything inappropriate, just vague insinuations. And your work was so thorough, so well-documented, that even his speculation couldn't touch it." Elliot takes a step toward me. "They accepted the assessment. All of it. Because you made it impossible for anyone to question the quality of your work, even if they questioned your relationship with me."

I can barely breathe. "So Harrison—"

"Failed. Completely. He tried to use our relationship against us and it backfired because you were so rigorous, so objective, that the work spoke for itself." His voice is rough with emotion. "You protected both of us, Cassie. You knew this might happen and you made sure it wouldn't matter."

The tears I've been holding back start falling. "I had to. I couldn't let Harrison destroy your career because of me."

"That's why you left. Not to protect your career—to protect mine."

"Yes." It's barely a whisper.

"God, Cassie." He closes the distance between us in two strides. "I've been such an idiot. I spent three weeks being angry because I thought you were choosing your career over us. But you were choosing to protect me. You sacrificed what we had to keep me safe from Harrison."

"It was the right thing to do."

"No, it wasn't. Because I don't want a career that costs me you." His hands cup my face, making me look at him. "I don't want success if it means being this miserable. I don't want any of it without you."

"Elliot—"

"I love you. I'm in love with you. I have been for months." His thumbs brush away my tears. "I know this is complicated. I know we still have to figure out where we're going to live and how to handle the board and all the logistics. But I'm willing to deal with all of that if you are. I'm willing to risk everything for us."

This is the moment. The moment I should tell him about the baby. The moment I should explain that everything just got exponentially more complicated.

But the words stick in my throat because I'm terrified.

Terrified he'll think I trapped him. Terrified this will be too much. Terrified he came here ready to fight for a relationship and I'm about to tell him he's also going to be a father.

"You don't understand," I manage. "There's something—I have to tell you something first. Something that changes everything."

"Nothing changes how I feel about you."

"This will." I pull back from his touch, wrapping my arms around myself for protection. "Elliot, I'm pregnant."

He goes completely still. "What?"

"I'm pregnant. With your baby. I found out three days ago." The words are tumbling out now, faster than I can control them. "One of the condoms must have failed. Probably during Christmas week. I didn't even know until my mother made a comment and I realized I'd missed two periods. I took three tests. All positive. I'm eight weeks pregnant."

He's staring at me like he can't process what I'm saying. Like the words aren't making sense.

"You're pregnant," he repeats slowly.

"Yes."

"With my baby."

"Yes." I'm watching his face, trying to read his expression, terrified of what I'm going to see. "I know this changes everything. I know you came here with a plan and this wasn't part of it. But you deserved to know. I was going to call you, was trying to figure out how to tell you, but you showed up and—"

He kisses me.

It's not what I expected. Not the reaction I was bracing for. But his mouth is on mine and his hands are in my hair and he's kissing me like I'm oxygen and he's been suffocating.

I make a sound of surprise, then kiss him back, my hands gripping his shirt like he might disappear if I let go.

When we finally pull apart, we're both breathing hard.

"You're pregnant," he says again, like he's trying to make it real.

"I'm sorry. I know you didn't sign up for—"

"Don't apologize." His hands frame my face again. "Don't you dare apologize for this. Cassie, I came here to tell you I love you and I want a future with you. This—" One hand moves to rest gently on my stomach. "This just means our future starts sooner than we thought."

"You're not angry?"

"Angry?" His laugh is shaky, disbelieving. "I'm terrified. I'm overwhelmed. I have no idea what I'm doing or how to be a father or any of it." His eyes are bright with unshed tears. "But angry? Never. This is—god, Cassie, this is everything I didn't know I wanted."

I start crying again, but this time it's relief flooding through me so powerfully my knees feel weak.

"I've been so scared," I whisper. "So scared you'd think I did this on purpose or that I was trapping you or—"

"Stop." He pulls me into his arms, holding me so tightly I can barely breathe. "I know you. I know you wouldn't do that. This was an accident. A beautiful, terrifying, completely unplanned accident. And we're going to figure it out together."

"I don't know how. I don't know where we're going to live or how to handle the board or what to do about our careers—"

"We'll figure it out. One thing at a time." He pulls back

just enough to look at me. "But first I need you to tell me something. Tell me you feel the same. Tell me you love me and you want this—us, the baby, the messy complicated future we're going to have to build together."

I look at him—this man I've been in love with for months, this man I left to protect, this man who flew to Portland to fight for us even though I told him I was choosing my career.

"I love you," I say, and the words feel like coming home. "I've been in love with you since before Christmas and it terrified me. That's why I ran. Because I've never felt this way about anyone and it was so big and overwhelming and I didn't know how to handle it."

"So you decided to handle it by pushing me away and protecting my career instead of fighting for us?"

"Yes. Because I thought your career was more important than my feelings."

"It's not." His voice is fierce. "Nothing is more important than this. Than you. Than the family we're building." His hand is still on my stomach, protective and tender. "I love you, Cassie. I love you and I love this baby and I want to build a life with you even though I have no idea what that looks like yet."

"Me neither."

"Then we start there. With love and commitment and the determination to figure out the rest as we go." He kisses me again, softer this time. "We can do this. Together."

I want to believe him. Want to think that love is enough to overcome all the logistics and complications and impossible questions we're facing.

But I'm also terrified. Because I've spent my entire adult life making careful, rational decisions designed to protect myself from exactly this kind of vulnerability. And now I'm standing in my mother's living room pregnant with my former CEO's baby, crying and kissing him and promising to build a future I can't even imagine.

It's terrifying.

It's also the most right thing I've ever done.

"Okay," I whisper against his lips. "Okay. We'll figure it out together."

He smiles, that brilliant smile I fell in love with months ago, and kisses me again.

We stay like that for a long time—holding each other, kissing, crying a little, laughing at the absurdity of how we got here. When we finally pull apart, we're both calmer, more settled.

"We should probably talk about logistics," I say, trying to be practical even though my heart is still racing. "Where we're going to live, what we're going to tell people, how—"

"Later." He leads me to the couch and pulls me down beside him. "Right now I just want to sit here with you and process the fact that I'm going to be a father."

"Are you freaking out?"

"Completely." He laughs. "I'm CEO of a major company and I have no idea how to balance that with being a parent." He looks at me. "But I also know I want this. Want you. Want our baby. Everything else we'll learn as we go."

I lean my head on his shoulder, his arm coming around me automatically. "I still can't believe I was planning to do this alone. The whole single mother thing. I had it all mapped out—IUI in April, pregnancy over the summer, baby in winter. Very controlled. Very planned." I can't help but laugh at the absurdity. "My life has never been this chaotic."

He presses a kiss to my hair. "I like it better this way. Messy and unplanned and completely terrifying."

I laugh. "You say that now. Wait until we're sleep-deprived and covered in baby spit-up and have no idea what we're doing."

"We'll still have each other. That's what matters."

We sit in comfortable silence for a few minutes, just being together. Then Elliot says quietly, "I need to ask you something."

"Okay."

"Do you want to keep the baby?" He's watching me carefully. "I know you planned for single motherhood eventually, but this wasn't how you imagined it. If you're not ready—if you want other options—I'll support whatever you decide."

The question catches me off guard. Not because I haven't thought about it, but because I already know the answer with absolute certainty.

"I want this baby," I say firmly. "I wanted a baby before I even met you. This isn't how I planned it, and the timing is terrible, and everything's complicated. But yes. I want this baby. Your baby. Ours."

The relief on his face is palpable. "Good. That's—that's really good."

"Did you think I might not?"

"I didn't know. I didn't want to assume." He takes my hand, lacing our fingers together. "But I'm glad. Because I want this too. All of it. You and the baby and the chaos and the mess."

"Even though it means telling the board? Dealing with whatever complications come from the CEO having a baby with his former compliance officer?"

"Even then." He's quiet for a moment. "Though we

should probably talk about that. About what we're going to tell people and when."

"I'm only eight to nine weeks along," I say. "Most people wait until twelve weeks to announce."

"So we have a month before we need to tell anyone."

"Assuming I don't start showing before then." I glance down at my still-flat stomach. "And assuming we figure out what our relationship looks like to the outside world."

"What do you want it to look like?"

The question is simple but the answer is complicated. What do I want? A relationship with Elliot that's public and acknowledged? Or do we keep hiding, keep pretending we're just colleagues who happened to reconnect?

"I want to be with you," I say finally. "Openly. I'm tired of hiding and sneaking around and being careful about who might see us together."

"Good. Because I'm tired of that too." He shifts to face me more fully. "Here's what I'm thinking. We tell people we're together—not about the baby yet, but about the relationship. We frame it as something that developed after your contract ended, which is true in terms of when we can be public about it."

"Harrison will know that's not entirely accurate."

"Harrison suspects but can't prove anything. And even if he tries to raise doubts, your assessment already went through the board. It's accepted. Done. He missed his window to use our relationship against us."

"So we just—what? Start dating publicly?"

"We start building a life together. You move to LA, or I move to San Francisco, or we figure out something else entirely. We tell our families and friends. We stop hiding." He squeezes my hand. "And when we're ready, when you're past the first trimester and feeling more secure about the pregnancy, we tell people about the baby."

It sounds so simple when he says it like that. Like we can just decide to be together and everything else will fall into place.

But I know it won't be that easy. There will be questions from the board, speculation about when our relationship really started, concerns about my objectivity during the assessment. There will be logistics to figure out—careers and housing and childcare. There will be a thousand complications we haven't even thought of yet.

But looking at Elliot, seeing the love and determination in his eyes, I think maybe we can handle it. Maybe love and commitment are enough to build on, even when everything else is uncertain.

"Okay," I say. "Let's do it. Let's build a life together."

He kisses me, slow and deep and full of promise. When we pull apart, he's smiling.

"So," he says. "Where do you want to start?"

The door opens before I can answer and my mother appears, looking pleased with herself.

"So," she says, leaning on her cane. "Did you two figure everything out?"

"We're working on it," I say, standing up. Elliot stands too, his hand finding mine automatically.

My mother's eyes go to our joined hands, then to my face, and she smiles. "Good. I'm glad you stopped being stubborn."

"Mom—"

"Don't 'Mom' me. You were miserable for three weeks and I had to watch you cry yourself to sleep every night. I'm thrilled you finally told him how you feel." She looks at

Elliot. "You're staying for dinner, I hope? I want to get to know the father of my grandchild properly."

Elliot's eyes widen slightly. "You told her?"

"She figured it out," I say. "Apparently I was acting pregnant."

"You were acting heartbroken and hormonal," my mother corrects. "Which led me to the obvious conclusion." She settles into her recliner. "So, Elliot. Tell me about your plans with my only daughter."

And just like that, we're talking about plans and logistics and the future we're building together. It's surreal and over-whelming and nothing like I imagined my life would be.

Not the careful, controlled plan I had constructed. But this—messy and unplanned... and absolutely perfect.

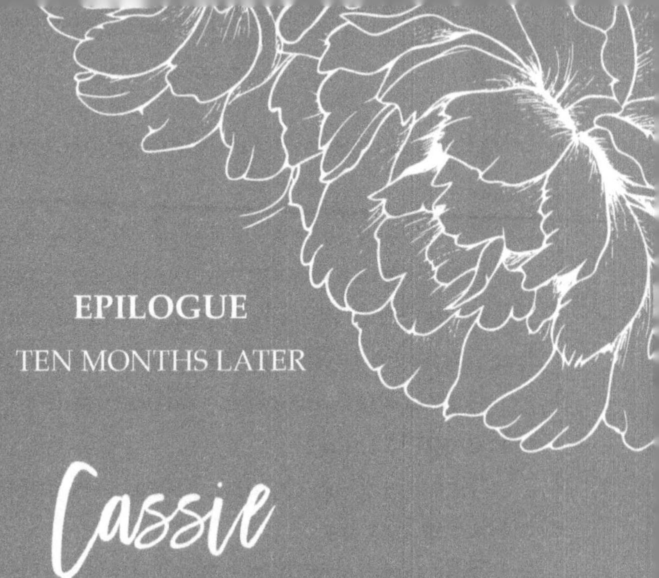

EPILOGUE

TEN MONTHS LATER

Cassie

THE NOVEMBER MORNING is cool and bright, sunlight streaming through the bedroom windows of the Eagle Rock house. I wake to the sound of Evelyn fussing in her bassinet —not crying yet, just those little warm-up noises that mean she'll be demanding to eat in the next five minutes.

One month old today. Four weeks since she came into the world screaming and perfect, with Elliot's dark hair and my nose and lungs that proved immediately she was not going to be a quiet baby.

I ease out of bed carefully, trying not to wake Elliot, but his hand catches mine.

"I've got her," he murmurs, already half-sitting up. "You sleep."

"You have to go to the office today."

"In two hours. I can handle a feeding." He's already moving to the bassinet, scooping up our daughter with the easy confidence he's developed over the past month. "Good morning, Evie girl. Are you hungry?"

She responds with an indignant squawk that makes me smile.

"I'm awake anyway," I say, sitting up. "Hand her over."

Elliot settles beside me on the bed, passing Evelyn into my arms. She's already rooting around, impatient, and I get her latched on while Elliot watches with that expression he gets sometimes—wonder and love and slight disbelief that this is our life now.

"She's getting so big," he says, running a gentle finger along her tiny fist.

"She's one month old. She's supposed to get bigger."

"I know. But I want her to stay small for a little bit longer." He leans over to kiss Evelyn's head, then mine. "How are you feeling?"

"Tired. Sore. Completely in love with both of you." I lean into him. "Happy."

"Good." He wraps an arm around us both, and we sit like that while Evelyn eats—our little family in the quiet morning light.

This wasn't the plan. A year ago, I was preparing to pursue single motherhood. I had it all mapped out—controlled, careful, on my own terms. I was going to do it alone because that felt safer than risking my heart on someone who might leave.

And then Elliot walked into my life—or back into it, really—and turned every careful plan upside down.

Now we're married, raising our daughter, building a life I never imagined wanting.

And I've never been happier.

"What time are Declan and Maya coming?" Elliot asks.

"Around eleven. Maya wants to bring lunch so I don't have to cook."

"She's been amazing. They both have."

He's right. Declan and Maya have been constant presences over the past month—bringing meals, offering to hold Evelyn so we could shower or nap, generally being the kind of family support that makes new parenthood slightly less overwhelming.

Elliot's whole family has been wonderful, actually. Keeley visits twice a week with her kids, bringing meals and offering to hold Evelyn so I can rest. His father has mellowed into a doting grandfather who holds Evelyn like she's made of glass and tells her stories about her grandmother who would have loved her. Even his sisters have been supportive —more calls and visits in the past month than in the previous year combined.

My mother flew down from Portland two weeks ago and stayed for five days, helping with laundry and cooking and teaching me everything she remembered about caring for a newborn. She cried when she held Evelyn for the first time —happy tears, she insisted, because her daughter finally has everything she deserves.

Lauren flew down from San Francisco the week after Evelyn was born, took one look at me exhausted and overwhelmed, and immediately took charge. She organized the kitchen, labeled all the baby supplies, set up a meal delivery schedule, and held Evelyn for three hours straight so I could sleep. Before she left, she made me promise to call her every week, not because she was worried but because she wanted to be part of Evelyn's life.

'You're my family,' she said. 'Which makes this little one my family too. I expect regular photos and video calls and for her to know her Aunt Lauren.'

She's already sent four packages of baby clothes.

The board at Pierce handled the pregnancy announce-ment better than I expected. We told them in May, after I was safely past the first trimester. Elliot framed it simply: we'd developed a relationship after my contract ended, I was pregnant, we were building a life together.

There were questions, of course. A few raised eyebrows. Harrison Gordon made some noise about the timeline being suspicious, but with my assessment already accepted and my employment ended, there wasn't much he could do except look petty.

Melinda pulled Elliot aside after the announcement and told him quietly that she was happy for him, that it was clear he and I were good for each other, and that she expected him to take appropriate paternity leave when the baby arrived.

He did. Three full weeks in October, right after Evelyn was born. Three weeks of him being home with us, learning to change diapers and soothe a crying baby and function on two hours of sleep. Three weeks of building our family together.

Though we have a housekeeper who comes in three days a week, I love staying home. I love being a wife and mother.

Now Elliot's back at work, but only for partial days. He comes home by three PM every afternoon, takes over baby duty so I can shower or nap or just have a moment to myself, and refuses to take evening calls unless there's an actual emergency.

"I have a family now," he told Colton when his CFO questioned the reduced schedule. "Pierce will survive if I'm not available 24/7."

Colton just smiled and said, "Good man. Enjoy it while she's little."

Evelyn finishes eating and I lift her to my shoulder for burping, patting her back gently while she makes those little grunting noises that still amaze me. A month ago, this tiny person didn't exist outside my body. Now she's here, real and perfect and completely dependent on us for everything.

"I still can't believe we made her," Elliot says, reading my mind.

"Technically we made her by accident while having sex over Christmas."

"Best accident of my life." He's watching Evelyn with that soft expression again. "I keep thinking about how different everything could have been. If that condom hadn't failed. If you hadn't gotten pregnant. If you'd stuck to your original plan and done the IUI alone."

"I'd have a baby. But not this baby. And not you." I lean my head on his shoulder. "I thought I wanted to do it alone. Thought that was safer, more controlled. But this—having you, having our family—it's so much better than anything I planned."

"Even though it's chaos?"

"Especially because it's chaos." I smile. "Turns out I'm okay with things not going according to plan. As long as you're here."

Evelyn lets out a satisfying burp, and we both laugh.

"She's definitely your daughter," Elliot says. "No shame, complete confidence."

"She gets that from both of us."

We spend the next hour in the easy routine we've developed—Elliot changes Evelyn's diaper while I shower, then I take her downstairs while he gets ready for work. The house smells like coffee and the November air coming through the open kitchen windows.

I settle on the patio with Evelyn in my arms, looking out at the garden. It's thriving—the terraced beds we worked on together last Christmas are lush and healthy, ready for winter. The bougainvillea is under control, the sage plants are shaped and fragrant, the whole space looks loved and tended.

Elliot's mother would be proud.

"Your grandmother would have loved you," I tell Evelyn softly. "She would have spoiled you rotten and taught you how to garden and told you stories about her mother in El Salvador."

Evelyn yawns, unimpressed by my philosophical musings, and I smile.

Elliot appears on the patio, dressed for work but still barefoot. "I have to leave in ten minutes. Can I hold her?"

I pass Evelyn over and he settles into the chair beside me, cradling our daughter against his chest. She fits perfectly there, tiny and safe in her father's arms.

"I don't want to go to work," he says. "I want to stay here with both of you all day."

"You can come home early."

"I will. Two PM at the latest." He kisses Evelyn's head. "Be good for your mama, Evie. No crying marathons while I'm gone."

As if on cue, Evelyn starts fussing, and Elliot looks betrayed.

"She knows I'm leaving. She's punishing me."

"She's one month old. She doesn't have that level of manipulation yet. Give her a few years."

He hands Evelyn back to me and she settles immediately, proving his point.

"See? She loves you more."

"She needs me more right now. You're her favorite for playtime." I stand, swaying slightly to keep Evelyn calm. "Go to work. We'll be here when you get back."

He kisses me, long and sweet, then kisses Evelyn's head again.

"I love you both," he says. "More than anything."

"We love you too. Now go run your company so you can come home and change diapers."

After he leaves, I spend the morning in the comfortable rhythm of new motherhood—feeding, changing, holding, rocking. Evelyn sleeps for an hour around ten, and I use the time to shower again and make myself look slightly more presentable before Declan and Maya arrive.

They show up at eleven on the dot, Maya carrying bags of food and Declan holding a wrapped package.

"How's our goddaughter?" Maya asks, immediately reaching for Evelyn, who's awake and alert in my arms.

"Perfect. Exhausting. Wonderful." I hand Evelyn over and Maya cradles her with the easy competence of someone who's been around babies before.

"She's gotten so big!" Maya coos. "Look at those cheeks. Declan, look at those cheeks."

Declan peers at Evelyn with the slightly wary expression of someone who's still not entirely comfortable with infants. "She looks the same as last week."

"She's grown at least half an inch and gained several ounces. It's very obvious." Maya is completely absorbed in Evelyn now, making silly faces that somehow our daughter finds fascinating.

"I brought lunch," Declan says, holding up a bag. "Thai food from that place you like."

"You're a saint." I lead them to the kitchen and we settle

around the table—Maya still holding Evelyn, Declan unpacking containers of pad thai and spring rolls, me finally eating something that isn't grabbed between baby care sessions.

"So," Maya says, looking up from making faces at Evelyn. "Elliot mentioned you're thinking about having her baptized?"

"We are. Probably sometime in December, before the holidays get too crazy." I take a bite of pad thai. "We wanted to ask you both something, actually."

Declan and Maya exchange a glance.

"We'd like you to be Evelyn's godparents," I say. "If you're willing. You've been such amazing support since she was born, and we can't think of anyone we'd trust more with her if something happened to us."

Maya's eyes fill with tears. "Really?"

"Really. You're family. The best kind of family—the kind we choose."

"We'd be honored," Declan says, his voice rougher than usual. "Truly honored."

Maya is crying now, still holding Evelyn carefully. "I promise we'll be the best godparents. We'll spoil her and teach her things and be there for all the important moments—"

"And keep her away from any terrible boyfriends when she's a teenager," Declan adds.

"She's one month old. Can we not talk about boyfriends yet?" But I'm smiling.

We spend the next hour eating and talking and passing Evelyn around. Declan tells stories about Elliot as a kid that make me laugh. Maya updates me on Highland Community Center news—they're expanding their programs and she's been working eighty-hour weeks trying to manage it all.

"You're going to burn out," I warn her.

"Says the woman who hasn't slept more than two hours at a stretch in a month," Maya counters.

"That's different. I'm caring for a newborn. You're choosing to work yourself to death."

"She's right," Declan says. "I've been telling you the same thing for weeks."

Maya sighs. "I know. I just—there's so much to do and I want to make sure everything's done right."

"Delegate," I say. "Trust other people to carry the load. You don't have to do everything yourself."

It's advice I'm still learning to take myself. For twenty years I controlled every aspect of my career, my life, my plans. Now I'm learning to let Elliot help, to accept support from family and friends, to trust that I don't have to manage everything alone.

It's harder than it sounds. But also incredibly freeing.

"How are you doing?" Maya asks gently. "Really? Not just the standard 'I'm fine' answer."

I take a moment to really consider the question. How am I doing?

Physically, I'm exhausted. Sleep-deprived and sore and still recovering from childbirth. My body doesn't feel like my own yet, and I'm learning to be patient with the healing process.

Emotionally, I'm overwhelmed. The love I feel for Evelyn is so intense it's almost frightening. And my love for Elliot has deepened into something even more profound now that we're parents together.

But underneath all the exhaustion and overwhelm,

there's profound happiness. A sense of rightness. A feeling that I'm exactly where I'm supposed to be, doing exactly what I'm meant to do.

"I'm really good," I say honestly. "Tired, definitely. Sometimes I wonder what I've gotten myself into. But good. Really, really good."

"You look happy," Maya says. "Happier than I've ever seen you, actually."

"I am." I glance around the kitchen—this kitchen where Elliot and I cooked together last Christmas, where we've now prepared bottles and sterilized pacifiers and figured out how to function as parents. "This is what I wanted. I just didn't know it until it happened."

At least we have someone come in three times a week to clean the house. Elliot would have hired someone full-time but I like having some sort of control in our house.

Evelyn starts fussing in Maya's arms, that warning sound that means she's building up to a real cry.

"Someone's hungry again," I say, standing to take her.

"Three-hour schedule?" Maya asks.

"More like two and a half. She's very demanding."

I settle in the living room to feed Evelyn while Declan and Maya clean up lunch. When they're done, they join me on the couch, and we talk about the baptism—potential dates, who to invite, whether to have it at a church or somewhere more casual.

"His sisters will have opinions," I say. "Keeley's already texting me decoration ideas."

"Let her plan," Maya advises. "Enjoy having someone else manage the logistics for once."

More good advice I should probably take.

Declan and Maya leave around two, just before Elliot

gets home. He finds me in the garden, Evelyn asleep in my arms, sitting on the bench where we used to sit together and watch the sunset.

"This is my favorite sight," he says, settling beside me. "My two favorite people in our garden."

"Our garden. I like that."

"Well, you did half the work fixing it up. It's as much yours as mine, although I'm glad we finally found the right gardeners." He wraps an arm around my shoulders. "How was the visit with Declan and Maya?"

"Good. I asked them to be godparents. They said yes."

"Perfect. I can't think of better people." He peers at Evelyn's sleeping face. "How's she been?"

"Fussy around noon, but she's been asleep for almost an hour now. Which means she'll probably be up all night."

"Then we better nap while we can."

We sit in the garden for a while longer, just the three of us, watching the afternoon light filter through the trees. The house behind us is full of our life together—Evelyn's nursery in what used to be Elliot's office, baby gear scattered throughout every room, evidence of the chaos and joy of new parenthood everywhere.

This house used to feel like something I was visiting. A place I stayed but didn't belong.

Now it feels like home.

"I was thinking," Elliot says quietly. "About how different everything is from a year ago. Last year, I was stressed about the CEO transition and worried about Harrison and trying to figure out how to handle the compliance assessment that was coming."

"And I was in San Francisco planning my fertility treatments and convinced I was going to do everything alone."

"And now look at us."

"Now look at us," I echo. "Living together. Raising our daughter. Building something I never imagined wanting."

"Are you happy?" He asks it like he's not quite sure, like he needs to hear me say it.

"Elliot, I'm happier than I've ever been in my life. This —" I gesture at Evelyn, at the garden, at the house behind us. "This is everything I wanted. I just didn't know it until I had it."

He kisses my temple. "I love you. Both of you. More than I knew it was possible to love anyone."

"We love you too."

Evelyn stirs in my arms, making those little sounds that mean she's waking up. In a minute she'll want to eat again, or need a diaper change, or just want to be held and talked to.

In a minute, the evening routine will start—dinner and baths and the endless cycle of feeding and changing and soothing that defines our days now.

But for this moment, we're just the three of us in the garden. Our family. Our home. Our perfectly imperfect life that started with a failed condom and a compliance assessment and two people who were too scared to admit they were falling in love.

I wouldn't change any of it.

Not the complications or the fear or the messy, unplanned way we got here.

Because it led us exactly where we needed to be.

Together.

Thank you so much for reading Cassie and Elliot's story! I hope you enjoyed watching them navigate the complicated path from mentor and student to lovers, and finally to the family they built together.

If you loved their story, sign up for my newsletter and receive an exclusive bonus scene—Practice Makes Perfect—featuring Cassie and Elliot's romantic getaway one year after Evelyn's birth. It's steamy, sweet, and shows them reconnecting as a couple while navigating new parenthood.

By signing up for my newsletter, you'll also receive updates on new releases, exclusive content, and behind-the-scenes glimpses into upcoming stories.

If you're curious about how this all began, I invite you to discover the other books in the Worth It All series:

***Worth the Risk** follows Declan and Maya's story—the foundation that brought this world to life. You'll see how Highland Community Center became Maya's passion project, and witness the relationship that Elliot watched unfold (and that eventually inspired him to take his own risks).*

***Worth the Wait** introduces you to Maya's best friend Lianne and the billionaire who wants a second chance.*
You can find both books and explore the complete series on Worth It All series page.

*Colton has his own story, too, in **Unwrapping Cole**, coming soon this holiday season.*

OTHER BOOKS BY LIZ DURANO

<u>Different Kind of Love: Taos</u>

Everything She Ever Wanted

Breaking the Rules

Where She Belongs

Other Side of Love (Prequel)

<u>Different Kind of Love: New York</u>

Falling for Jordan

Friends with Benefits

Lucky Charm

<u>Love Beach Ever After</u>

Summer with a Navy SEAL

Merry with a Tycoon

Spring Break with a Bodyguard

<u>Celebrity</u>

Loving Ashe

Loving Riley

<u>Holiday Engagement</u>

The Replacement Fiance

The Reluctant Fiancee

ABOUT THE AUTHOR

Although Liz studied Journalism in college, she discovered that she preferred writing fiction over ad copy, and so these days, she writes women's fiction and romance.

She lives in Southern California with her family and a senior Chihuahua mix who keeps guard of her writing space and a growing pile of books (and wool for when she needs to spin for inspiration).

You can follow Liz's book adventures by visiting lizdurano.com

facebook.com/lizduranobooks
instagram.com/lizdurano
bookbub.com/authors/liz-durano